STRANGER A

Follyfoot books by Monica Dickens

Follyfoot
Dora at Follyfoot
The Horses at Follyfoot
Stranger at Follyfoot

MONICA DICKENS

STRANGER AT
FOLLYFOOT

HEINEMANN : LONDON

William Heinemann Ltd
Michelin House
81 Fulham Road,
London SW3 6RB

LONDON   MELBOURNE   AUCKLAND

First published 1976
© Monica Dickens 1976
Reprinted 1988
0 434 93464 X

Printed in Great Britain by
Richard Clay Ltd
Bungay, Suffolk

I

'THAT horse,' Steve said, 'is leading the life of a spoiled child.'

'He is only a child.' Dora had tied the colt Folly to a ring in a post, and was going over him with one of Anna's old silk scarves. It made his brown coat shine like the burnished chestnuts on the trees which stood on either side of the gate into Follyfoot. 'He's only two. Fourteen in human counting.' She walked after him as he danced round the post.

'When I was fourteen,' Steve said, 'I was sent out to work. Folly should have been backed by now.'

'Callie's been dying to get on him, but the Colonel said not yet. He's small, Steve.'

'He's a firecracker.' Steve took hold of the rope near the halter to hold the restless colt still. 'The Colonel thought he'd be too much for Callie, but if you told her that, she'd be on him in a flash.'

'I don't know,' Dora said. 'She's a bit nervous really.'

'That's just it. Nervous people make themselves do things.'

Dora looked at him quickly. How could Steve know that? He wasn't afraid of anything.

'Callie won't be back from school till four,' Steve said. 'Come on, Dora, let's get some weight on his back. See how he takes to it. Born to work, this little devil is. He's going to love it.'

'Callie will be furious.'

'She won't know. We'll start working with him while she's at school, and when we suggest to her she gets on him, he won't give her any trouble.'

Folly had already got used to a mouthing bit, with loose

metal pieces to teach him to flex his neck and play with the bit. Steve put the mouthing bridle on him, and his headcollar over it with a long lungeing rein, and took him out into the small field behind the Dutch barn. It was the best lungeing place, since it was enclosed, and was without the distraction of the other horses grazing or staring or jeering, or wandering up to interfere.

Dora shut the gate. She had had some experience with Folly dragging the rein through her hands and racing back to the stable, winding the long rein round wheelbarrows and other horses' legs as he went.

Before they put any weight on his back, they worked him in circles, enjoying the way he flexed to the mouthing bit, and the springy, supple paces that were going to make him a lovely ride. He could already walk, trot and canter to voice commands, and would stop dead if you yelled, 'Whoa!', and stand on the outside of the circle, instead of nipping into the middle like Dora's horse Robin, to see what was in your pocket.

Callie had done a fine job with Folly. He was going to reward her by being her dream horse one day, as Robin was Dora's.

'Now old man,' Steve said, 'we're going to show you why God made horses this shape.'

He had stuffed a sack with straw. It wasn't heavy, but it was bulky. Very carefully, Steve laid it across the colt's short back. Folly twitched, and flicked his short curved ears back and forth, but he stood still. Across the top of the straw-filled sack, Steve laid the narrow canvas surcingle that Callie's father had used with his racing saddle.

'Hang on to him now,' he told Dora, and gently, watching Folly's ears, began to draw it tight.

'All right, old man. Walk on.'

Dora went back to the middle of the circle, paying out the rein, and bent to make the gesture of picking up earth to throw, which was all Folly needed to make him move ahead. He walked, humping his back, and turning his head to see what he was carrying.

'Ter-rot!'

When he trotted, the sack bumped on his back. He bucked a few times, stopped dead, prodded the sack with his nose, snorted, kicked out, and then decided to trot out smoothly, carrying the sack like an old hand. It did seem as if he was, as Steve said, born to work.

'Let's try a saddle,' Dora said.

'It's too soon.'

'It's not. He's a natural. He's the best young horse we've ever worked with.'

They put a light saddle on the colt, not too tightly girthed. Folly rolled his eye and flicked his ears, but stood quietly.

'I'm going to get on him,' Dora said.

'Don't be an idiot. He's not nearly ready. You do it step by step. Get him used to weight gradually. It takes weeks.'

'Don't be such an old woman.' Dora was excited and impatient. 'You hold his head. I'm getting on.'

'He'll dump you.'

'I'll risk it.'

First she put her arms across the saddle, and leaned on the colt's back. He moved away and she followed, keeping her weight on him. Then she stood back, put her foot in the stirrup, and slowly put her weight on it.

Folly laid back his ears.

'Give him a break,' Steve said. 'It's too soon.'

'Sooner we do it,' Dora watched the colt's ears, 'sooner

3

Callie can get on him. And we'll let her think she's the first.'

'Get on with it then,' Steve said, 'or she'll be home from school.'

'Not for ages yet.' Dora settled herself in the saddle as gently as an egg. 'Walk him forward, Steve.'

2

THEY had reckoned without the local bus drivers. They called a strike on late buses, and people like Callie who lived at the top of the hill came home on an early bus.

It dropped Callie at the farm gate just as Steve let go of the headcollar and Dora gently squeezed Folly into a trot. At the first bounce of her muscular bottom, the colt squealed, put down his head and gave a neat, but powerful buck. Dora flew through the air and landed in a patch of long grass and thistles.

Folly gave another buck, to make sure he had got rid of her, tore off round the field with the reins over his head, went down and rolled to try and get rid of the saddle, caught the headcollar on a root, broke it, got up, shook himself and stood quietly with the saddle upside down underneath him.

'What are you doing with my horse?'

Callie came dashing round the barn, pigtails flying, casting off hat, satchel and blazer as she ran.

'Nothing.' Dora limped out of the long grass, rubbing her hip. 'It's what is he doing to me?'

'You must be doing something wrong.' Callie climbed the gate, and went slowly up to Folly with her hands behind her back, so that he wouldn't know he was going to be caught. She took off the broken headcollar, undid the girths and took off the saddle. She led him over to the gate, climbed on to it and eased herself gently on to his narrow back.

'Watch it,' Steve called, running towards the colt. 'He'll buck you off.'

'No, he won't. I've been riding him bareback for days, before any of you were up. I was going to surprise you.'

5

Steve stopped. He and Dora looked at each other and spread their hands helplessly.

'I thought the Colonel told you not to back him yet,' Dora said.

'Why were you doing it then?'

Callie grinned at them and rode in a rather wavering line towards the gate that led into the long hill pasture. Dora picked up the broken headcollar and went to open the gate. She watched as Callie rode the colt down through the field where some of the Follyfoot horses were pottering about their small daily affairs at the far end by the stream. Callie steered him round trees, trotted him on the flat ground, stopped him when he got excited, then turned and trotted back up the slope, hanging on to his mane as he peered and side-stepped at familiar stones and bushes he had been grazing among all his life.

'Isn't he perfect?' Callie slid off his back, and Folly immediately dropped his nose into her hand for the horse nuts she always carried in a pocket, whether she was in school uniform or not.

One day in Social Studies class, the teacher had asked everyone to empty their pockets to see what items were necessary to human beings. Most people had money and sweets and keys and old bus tickets and filthy handkerchiefs. Callie had horse nuts, horseshoe nails, a torn newspaper picture of a showjumper, and three inches she had cut off the end of Folly's tail to keep it out of the mud.

When she took off Folly's bridle, he galloped down the hill and across the stream to the other horses. Some of them, like Nigger and Dolly, who were irritated by the young, ignored him. Others raised their heads as he went up to them and exchanged news by nose, and a few comradely nips on the neck.

Dora went into the field to see Robin, the bay half thorough-

6

bred, half quarterhorse she had brought back from America. He came up to lay his nose against her cheek. He wasn't a greedy horse, like Cobbler's Dream, who was bumping his nose against the closed fists that Steve held out to tease him.

'O.K., Cobby, which hand?'

The chestnut pony smelled both hands, and then tried to pry open the fingers that held the horse nuts.

It was a beautiful autumn afternoon, warm, with the sun low in a sky that was a much deeper blue than in the summer. The green of the woodland was turning to yellows and oranges and reds before the leaves fell. The air was full of good autumn smells of fruit and bonfires. It was one of those last precious days to treasure before you wake one morning to frost on the window and the knowledge that in spite of your belief that summer will go on for ever, winter is here and you can't find last year's gloves.

Dora and Steve moved among the old horses, each of whom had a history of bad luck or cruelty which had brought them to spend their last days in peace at Follyfoot.

The spotted circus horse with a back as flat as a table from years of being danced on by ladies in spangles and rosined shoes. Hero, the other circus horse, whom Callie had rescued by stealing. Ginger from the old days of milk carts, Folly's mother Specs from the junkyard, Amigo, the pale bony horse who would have been sold to die in harness if Dora had not bought him at an auction. Dottie the donkey with her foal Polka Dot who had been born unexpectedly under a hedge in the rain. Dear old Stroller, and Ranger, and Frank, and the Weaver, all the old friends.

3

THE dong dong of the big bell outside the stables was Slugger telling them to come back and start the evening's work.

Dora and Steve and Callie walked up the hill on the cropped turf, ahead of them the low, solid farm buildings and the well known umbrella shapes of the elms that punctuated the hedge along the road.

At the top of the field, they turned, as they always did, and leaned on the gate to look back at the horses grazing peacefully in the slanted sun that turned Robin's coat to a coppery red.

'I do love this place,' Dora sighed. 'I'm going to live here for ever and ever.'

Steve shrugged his shoulders. 'Nothing's certain.'

'If I want to stay here,' Dora said, 'I'll stay here.'

'Well,' Steve said, '*you* might be here, but the horses might not.'

'There'll always be horses at Follyfoot.' Dora turned and began to walk up the grassy track towards the stable yard.

'Things are getting pretty tough, you know.' Steve walked beside her with a serious face. 'The price of feed and hay and bedding goes up all the time.'

'It'll be all right.' Dora did not worry about money, because she never had any. 'It always is.'

'I suppose so,' Steve said. 'But it seems to be more of a headache. Haven't you noticed how quiet the Colonel is lately?'

'He's always quiet.'

The Colonel was a peaceful man of few words. He communicated best with horses, in a language of comfortable grunts and murmurs and low whistles.

8

'More so than usual.' Steve frowned. 'I said yesterday, "Colonel, if we plough up that bare corner by the wood and resow it, in two years' time, we'll have a beautiful stand of hay." Normally he'd say, "Go ahead and do it." Yesterday he just sort of patted me on the shoulder in an absent-minded way and said, "Let's not make too many long range plans."'

As they rounded the corner of the loose boxes and came into the cobbled yard, where hay seeds had lodged among the cobbles and sprouted friendly tufts of grass, the Colonel came out of Ginger's box. He was wearing the apron with the deep pockets which held hoof picks, brushes, bandages, bottles of embrocation.

'Hullo, Colonel.'

He gave Dora the jerky nod with which he acknowledged greetings.

'How's Ginger's leg?'

'So-so.' He and Dora looked over the door of the box where the old milk horse stood in a corner with his left forefoot in a poultice of hot bran in sacking tied round the leg with string.

His belly sagged behind the bony shoulder blades. His hips stuck out like a coat hanger. He had lost all the hair from the top of his tail by rubbing it against his favourite tree. Parts of his wispy mane had gone the same way. There were bare places on his coat where some of the younger horses had nipped at him. He looked like a family's well-used, moth-eaten rocking horse, abandoned in the corner of a dusty attic. He was one of more than twenty four-legged reasons why there would always have to be horses at Follyfoot.

4

DORA started to clean out the loose boxes on her side of the yard. The forecast was for rain tonight. They might have to bring some of the older horses in.

As she took the wheelbarrow out to the Dutch barn to get another bale of straw, a car coming down the road slowed, then stopped outside the gate with the sign, 'Home of Rest for Horses'.

It was a small dusty car, ill-cared for. A man got out and came through the gate to where Dora was heaving down a bale of straw from the stack.

'Let me help you.'

'I'm fine.' Dora thought she was probably stronger than he was. He looked like a city person, with his dark suit, black shoes and narrow tie. Close up, the suit was rumpled, the shoes worn, the tie and shirt collar frayed.

'Is this the Home of Rest for Horses?' he asked, although he must have read it on the board at the gate.

Dora nodded, brushing straw from the front of her sweater.

'I've come,' the man said, 'to ask if you could take my horse.'

'I hope so,' Dora smiled. Although she had more than twenty horses to take care of, the idea of a new one was always pleasing.

'It's like this, you see,' the man said. 'I'm going away. To South America, as a matter of fact. Got the chance of a job there with a friend of mine.'

'I've been to America,' Dora said. She had stayed with the Colonel's friend Mr Blankenheimer, who dreamed of starting a Follyfoot Farm in the United States. 'That's where I got my bay horse Robin. He's half quarter –'

The man was not listening. 'Got to make a new start, you see.' He spoke half to himself. 'Things haven't worked out for me here. It's all got to go. The factory. The house. And worst of all – Kingfisher.'

'What kind of a horse is he?'

'Well . . . I don't know. Just a horse,' the man said vaguely. 'He's sort of a mottled colour, freckled, and thick in the middle. Very gentle. I don't know much about horses and riding, but I feed him and brush him and give him sugar treats, and we have lovely trots round the roads. The King has taught me all I know.'

Which isn't much, Dora thought.

'He's been a good friend to me.' The man's face was creased with anxiety. His eyes dropped like a bloodhound. 'That's why I'd like to bring him here. I couldn't have him – you know – put away, but I can't afford to pay anyone for his keep. There's a riding stable in the suburb where I live that might buy him, but he's too old to work like that, and his legs swell up and he's a little nippy until he gets to know you.'

Dora thought, *No wonder, if you feed him sugar and pound him round suburban streets*. But she said. 'Perhaps we could take him,' her mind already switching horses about so that Kingfisher could have the loose box with the bars where he could not nip at unwary visitors. 'Come and talk to the Colonel.'

'Let me help.' The man bent to wheel the barrow. The heavy bale of straw was badly balanced. The barrow swerved, the bale fell off, Dora heaved it on again and the man let her wheel it under the brick archway into the stable yard.

The Colonel was in the tack room, looking at Folly's broken headcollar.

'How did this happen?' He hated broken tack.

'Oh, well . . . he caught it on something.'

'How?'

Dora did not want an inquisition on the headcollar, with the man in the frayed tie hovering behind her, so she said, 'This is Mr – um.'

The Colonel turned. The man said, 'Ellis Elkins,' and held out his hand. The Colonel automatically wiped his hand on the side of his corduroys and shook hands.

'He's got this old horse, you see,' Dora said eagerly. 'He can't keep him any longer, and he can't sell him because of his legs, and I thought perhaps if we moved Ranger into Fanny's box, and put Fanny into that empty –'

'Whoa,' said the Colonel, and to Ellis Elkins, 'I'm sorry. We haven't any room, except for emergencies.'

'But there's that empty –'

The Colonel was too polite to say, 'Shut up,' but he gave Dora a look which said it for him, and she shut.

'You won't take Kingfisher?' Ellis Elkins looked blank.

'I can't.'

Dora went out of the tack room. She did not want to hear any more. Elkins stayed talking to the Colonel for a while longer, and he came out and walked towards his car with his shoulders bent and his hands in his pockets, kicking a pebble.

Dora called goodbye, but he got into his dusty car without looking back, and drove away.

'Dora!' Steve called. 'I thought you were getting me some bedding.'

'Get it yourself!' She went into Ginger's stable, because he was the only horse who was not out in the fields, and she needed a horse's neck to brood on. Things were happening at Follyfoot that she did not like.

5

SHE was still angry when she woke next day. She grumbled at the chickens pecking hopefully round the back doorstep. When she took in Stroller's feed, she pushed the heavy horse over more roughly than usual, then swore at one of the donkeys for standing on her toe, although its little shell foot did not hurt.

At breakfast in the kitchen, Callie, who had been up long before anyone else to ride Folly, came in fresh-faced, babbling about the marvels of the brown colt.

'Give it a rest,' Dora growled. 'You'd think he was the only horse in this place.'

'What's the matter, Dora?' Callie's mother Anna turned from the stove in surprise.

'Leave me alone.' Dora buttered toast savagely.

'She's crossed in love, that's what it is,' Ron Stryker said. 'I seen her talking to that bloke by the straw stack. Very fancy car, he had. Custom made scratches, painted in dust colour, them fashionable dented bumpers.'

Dora was torn between wanting to finish her breakfast, or leaving the room. She compromised by bolting down the rest of her sausage and eggs – 'Eats like a horse,' from Ron – wiping her mouth on the back of her hand – 'Man-*ners*!' – banging her chair back into the fireplace – 'Don't take it out on the furniture!' – and slamming out of the room – 'Nice knowin' yer.'

In the doorway, Dora collided with the Colonel, coming in with a serious face.

'I'm calling a staff meeting,' he said. 'In my study at eleven o'clock. I want you all there.'

'I've got to go to town to get that part for the pump,' Steve said.

'It can wait. I want everybody there.'

'Can I miss school?' Callie looked up hopefully.

'I don't mean you, Cal.'

She kicked the table leg. 'I miss all the fun.'

'This isn't –' the Colonel looked at Anna and swallowed – 'exactly fun.'

It was not fun.

One by one, they came in to the Colonel's shabby, comfortable study, and settled themselves in various places.

The Colonel sat sideways at his littered desk, his long legs crossed, his unlit pipe in his mouth. He still coughed, even when it was not lit.

Slugger, who had worked at the Farm since the Colonel came here, sat in the chair by the fire, dwarfed by the high back and the deep seat, which left his boots dangling short of the floor. His woollen cap, which was like hair to him, was still on top of his balding head.

Dora sat on the floor hugging her knees, the Colonel's yellow dog leaning against her, one of the cats criss-crossing under her legs.

Steve was on the couch with a lapful of puppies. Ron lounged on the windowsill.

The Colonel cleared his throat, and looked round the room.

'I've called this meeting,' he said, 'to talk about money.'

Groans all round.

'I may as well leave right now.' Dora pushed away the cat and began to stand up, 'since that's a subject I don't understand.'

'Shut up and sit down.' Steve leaned forward and pulled her back to the floor.

'As you know,' the Colonel went on, not looking at anybody, 'it's costing more every year to keep horses. A lot of stables have had to close. People have had horses put down. Some of them have sent their horses here.'

'Or tried to.' Dora was still sulking about Ellis Elkins.

'Some we've been able to take. Some we can't, if they seem reasonably fit. Like that man's horse yesterday, Dora. He –'

'You should have taken it. I thought that was what Follyfoot was *for*!'

'When we can afford it.'

'We've always managed somehow. We will again.'

'Oh belt up, Dora.' Steve poked her with his foot. 'Don't preach.'

'But I don't understand,' Dora said. 'I thought the whole idea of Follyfoot was to save horses at whatever cost.'

'To hear her talk,' Ron said, 'you'd think she'd invented this place. I was here for years before you came. Remember the day she came, Col? Walked into the yard in those weird clothes and said, "Do you ever hire girls?" Didn't know the north end of a horse from the south.'

'Don't change the subject,' the Colonel said. 'I've called this meeting because –'

He was interrupted again by a banging and a kind of snuffling sound outside the French window. Steve opened it. Dottie the chocolate donkey was waiting outside. She expanded her nostrils to the smell of the fire, then ambled in on her neat feet, bent her legs and flopped down on the hearthrug, with her ears laid contentedly sideways.

Dora shifted her position so that she could use the solid shoulder of the donkey for a back rest.

'Because,' the Colonel went on patiently, 'the Trustees of

the Farm have been after me to cut down on expenses. Where do I start? We can't skimp on feed and hay. I suppose we could save on bedding by leaving more horses out at night, but it's getting too cold for a lot of the old ones.'

They waited. They knew all this.

'The Trustees have told me,' the Colonel went on, 'that if we can't cut down on the horses, we – we'll have to ...' He stopped, bit at a nail, scratched his head, rubbed his cold pipe along his cheek, cleared his throat, 'cut down on staff.'

He said it apologetically, like a question, but there was no answer. Everyone was all of a sudden very busy. Dora was carefully picking flaky bits of scurf out of Dotty's wispy mane. Steve was trying to make the largest puppy's ears stand up, as they were supposed to do, if his father really was an Alsatian. Ron had picked up an old tennis racket from the corner and was strumming it, with his eyes on the ceiling. Slugger, sitting back behind the high sides of the chair where he could not see the Colonel, was investigating his ear with a matchstick.

The Colonel cleared his throat again. 'Well – what do you think?'

He looked round the room. No one would help him out, so he had to add, 'It's either that, you see, or we may have to put down some of the old horses.'

The reaction was immediate and unanimous.

'You can't do that,' Steve said.

'No way, Col,' from Ron.

'Oh please – no,' Dora said.

Slugger shook his head and muttered, 'It's not right, Colonel. Be against everything that Follyfoot stands for.'

'Well then.' The Colonel sighed. 'We will have to agree with the Board of Trustees and cut down on staff. Someone will have to go.'

Dora said, 'We'll work for nothing. I will, at least. I've told you that a thousand times.'

'And I've told *you* a thousand times I can't let you do that,' the Colonel said. 'You'd –' he made a face, as if the words hurt him – 'you'd have to get yourself another job.'

'What as?'

'In another stable.'

'Who'd have me?'

'You've had a lot of experience here.'

'We don't do things like other people.'

'Are you telling me,' the Colonel lowered his brows at her, 'that I'm not a good horse keeper?'

'I'm telling you that I think you're a better horse keeper than most people who keep horses. I'm not leaving anyway.' She stuck out her lip.

'Steve? Strong boy . . . get something else . . .' The Colonel's words were spoken in a strangled way, as if they were forced out of him in pain.

'With my record?' Steve had been in a lot of trouble before he came to Follyfoot with the pony Cobbler's Dream. 'I'm not going, Colonel, and that's flat.'

'Well, Ron will have to go.'

'You can't sack me,' Ron said, ''cos me uncle's your grain merchant, innee? That's why you took me on.' He faked a little tune on the tennis racket:

> *'You can't sack me,*
> *Cos if you sack me,*
> *You won't get cheap oats*
> *From me uncle, see?'*

'That's a point,' the Colonel said. 'Slugger?'

'Me!' Slugger sat up and peered round the edge of the chair

in outrage. 'I been here longer than anyone. Been with you right through the war, Colonel. Thick and thin. Pulled you out of that bomb shelter when the roof fell in. Nicked you a pair of boots that time yours rotted in the rain. Got you away from that blonde woman in Brussels . . .'

Ron let out a wolf whistle and the Colonel said, 'That's enough.'

Nothing was resolved. They looked at each other miserably. To their great relief, Anna knocked on the door.

'Sorry to interrupt the meeting.' She put her head round the door. 'Mrs Oldcastle just rang up. She says there's a horse in her vegetable garden and she's sure it's one of ours.'

Everyone jumped up.

'We haven't decided anything,' the Colonel said. 'Wait –' But they had all rushed out of the door.

6

THEY spread in different directions, to check on the horses in the various fields. They met again in the yard.

'It's not one of ours,' Dora said. 'We'd better go and find out whose it is.'

'Not our business,' Ron said.

'Any horse is our business, especially if it's loose in someone's vegetable garden.'

Dora wanted to take Robin out anyway. After the distressing scene in the Colonel's study, she was longing to get back to the realities of life, the simple joy of riding Robin. 'Coming, Steve?'

'All right.'

'Ron?'

'May as well. Nothing to do here but mucking out.'

They brought in Robin and Miss America and Hero, and put saddles and bridles on them without stopping to clean off the mud.

Slugger was mooching miserably about in the yard with his cap pulled over one eye.

'Come with us,' Dora said. 'You can ride Willy.'

'You must be barmy.'

'You used to ride in the Army, you know you did.'

'That was forty years ago,' Slugger said, 'when me legs was young. You won't catch me getting on a horse again.'

They clattered out of the yard, and rode without talking through the woods, across the main road, and down the narrow winding lane that led to the back entrance of Mrs Oldcastle's house.

It was a huge old house with turrets and many chimneys, and ivy crowding the walls as if it was trying to camouflage the house as part of the green landscape. Mrs Oldcastle's husband, who had died of big business, had left her plenty of money, but she lived alone in the rather creepy house, with priceless pictures and antiques, it was said, and a little dog and her old chestnut cob Harold for company.

Harold called from his ivy-hung stable as they came up the back drive from the lane. There was no sign of a loose horse.

'Hang on,' said Steve. 'Somebody had better get off and check for hoof prints before we make a lot more.'

He held Hero while Ron went to investigate.

'Tracks there all right,' Ron said coming back. 'They smashed the poor old lady's carrot tops and a row of brussels sprouts, which could be a good thing, according to taste.'

'Better go and ask her about the horse.'

In his cowboy hat and his pointed boots and decorated leather jacket, Ron went round the house to the front door. He wiped his boots on the scraper, rang the bell and heard no sound, and banged the big brass knocker.

Immediately there began a pulling of bolts and a turning of keys, as Mrs Oldcastle had been standing behind the door, peering through the stained glass lozenges of the side window. The heavy door opened. She was wearing an old green kimono, with her grey hair bundled into a sleeping net, but she received Ron as graciously as if she were fully dressed for dinner.

'I'm from Follyfoot.' Ron looked beyond her into the great shadowed hall, where a suit of armour stood like a metal butler, with a small silver tray held out in the fingers of its gauntlet.

'That's good,' said Mrs Oldcastle, in the breezy way which

matched her pink outdoor skin and cheerful blue eyes. 'Did you take your horse away?'

'It wasn't ours,' Ron said. 'None of ours is missing.'

'It's always one of yours,' Mrs Oldcastle said. 'They get out all the time.'

'No, lady, excuse *me*.' Ron's practised eye travelled round the hall, where dark portraits of the ancient dead looked down on carved chests and Chinese urns and porcelain figures and silver candlesticks. With all this stuff, she didn't need to be worrying about a few carrot tops and brussels sprouts. 'I detected hoofmarks there.' He gave her his sleuth look. 'But no horse.'

'But it's there. Among my sprouts. I saw it with my own eyes, a fleabitten grey, in a red webbing halter. Come and I'll show you.'

Ron followed the lumpy figure tied into the green kimono through the hall, down a panelled passage, through a pantry whose shelves were stacked with pieces of valuable china and blackened silver.

The kitchen beyond was cluttered with the debris of the old lady's random housekeeping. On the floor, a smug grey Persian cat lapped milk from a delicate flowered bowl.

'Go and look.' Mrs Oldcastle pointed at the window.

Ron looked out. He saw nothing except the vegetable garden, with Steve and Dora holding the horses off to one side.

'You see that grey horse? I know it's yours.'

She must be hallucinating. Ron said soothingly, 'Oh yes, I see it,' in case she was crazy and might attack him with a carving knife.

'Then you must be even more senile than me,' Mrs Oldcastle said tartly, joining him at the window, 'for now that I look again, it's gone. There's only that girl and whatsisname out there.'

Mrs Oldcastle waved to Steve and Dora, but they didn't see her, so she waved to Harold in his stable instead.

'Your grey may be anywhere by now. You'd better go after it.'

Ron said, 'All right,' which was easier than, 'We haven't got a fleabitten grey,' and accepted a rather stale chocolate cupcake, which she fished from a drawer full of string and rusted screws, tipped his ten gallon hat and followed her out through the pantry and the passage and the hall.

The sight of all the valuable stuff crammed into this house made Ron think about the unpleasant scene in the study, and the Colonel talking so unhappily about money. It didn't seem fair. As Mrs Oldcastle opened the front door, he managed to say, 'If you was ever thinking of making a donation to Folly-foot –'

'If you've come here to beg, young man,' she said ungratefully, since he had come here to help her, 'you've come to the wrong shop,' and Ron found himself out in the garden, with the heavy door swinging shut behind him with an aggressive, portcullis sound.

'Mean old devil.' He went back to the others, muttering, 'Wouldn't give you the dirt from under her nails. And she sees things too. Hallucinating.'

'But there are hoof tracks there,' Dora said. 'They go over the lawn to the front drive and then disappear.'

'You're hallucinating too.' Ron vaulted into Hero's saddle, which made the old horse stagger. 'Come on, I want me dinner.'

'We'd better look for the horse.' Dora walked Robin slowly down the drive, looking for tracks on either side.

'I'm going home.' Steve turned Miss America to follow Ron.

Normally he would have stayed with Dora, but he was

depressed by what the Colonel had said. He had meant it. Things were serious. As he jogged past Ron and trotted ahead, the Colonel's words kept going through his head.

Might have to cut down on staff . . .

And Steve knew who would have to go. The Colonel had taken him on as a favour, to keep him from trouble. Given him a home and a job. And a family. All right. So now it was over.

Ron kicked Hero in the ribs and galloped past Steve. He got home first, riding the horse too fast, and made it up by bringing him a feed of oats before he turned him out.

Life of Riley. Ron watched the horse grab at the feed, standing in deep straw in the comfortable loose box. Better off than some people Ron knew who lived in the bad areas of town, and down by the canal where Carter's coal yard was.

Ron grumbled about the work at Follyfoot, but at least he had a job, which was more than most of his mates had. If he lost this job, because of the money . . .

'Mean old devil.' He kicked the stable door, as if it were Mrs Oldcastle's portcullis. He was still angry with her.

7

Mrs Oldcastle's long front drive ran down to the road between tall pointed fir trees. Beyond them on either side was an expanse of good turf, where Mr Oldcastle had once kept prize cattle, but which was now grazed only by the ponderous cob Harold.

After Steve and Ron started for home, Dora went alone down the drive, looking right and left for the stray horse's tracks. She was tempted to look back to see if Steve had changed his mind and turned to follow her, but she humped her shoulders against the temptation, in case he was not following, but had turned to see whether she was looking to see if he was.

Rats, both of them, Steve and Ron. They were all supposed to be vigilantes for any horse in trouble, and a loose horse was always trouble, whoever it belonged to, with the main roads so busy, and drivers not caring.

Dora rode slowly, with the reins loose on Robin's neck. Steve going home was just one of the horrible things that seemed to be happening these days. She expected a few more before the week was out. If anyone had to be sacked, it was always the girl . . .

Halfway down the drive, she realized that there had been a trodden place between two fir trees, and turned Robin back to look. Large hoof marks – yes, going off into the thick turf. For a short while, she could see where the long wet grass had been brushed forward as the horse had moved in a rather wavering pattern – grazing perhaps – that soon became impossible to follow.

Dora pushed on Robin's neck to try to get him to put his head down.

'If you were a dog, you could track him.'

A bird flew suddenly up out of the grass. Robin jumped forward and set off in his beautiful smooth canter.

A shallow stream ran in a curly line half way across the meadow. If the horse had crossed it, it would be possible to trace him on the muddy banks. Dora started at the top end and followed its meandering course down towards the road. Robin jogged and fussed, wanting to canter again. When they found the trampled place where the horse had crossed, she jumped him over and let him go fast towards the hedge at the end of the grassland, which would be the next place where they could do any tracking.

The hedge ran from the road to the top of a slight hill. Even if the horse had jumped it clean, there would be hoof marks at the take-off. It was not until they were almost at the top of the slope that Dora saw broken branches where the hedge had been roughly pushed through by a cumbersome object that obviously didn't know much about jumping. A large lump of hedge had been pulled forward into the next field. A tuft of light hair and some grey tail hairs were clinging to a briar.

The next field was plough, so it was easy to tell where the horse had gone. Following the next furrow, Dora could see where the horse had walked, the fore and hind prints close together, and where he had trotted, with all four feet evenly spaced out.

At the end of the plough, a dry ditch led on to a road, and there she lost the tracks.

Down the road, a man was digging in a cottage garden.

Dora called to him, 'Did you see a loose horse go by here?'

'Fleabitten grey, kind of. Red halter. Chunky chap.'

'You couldn't catch him?'

'Going too fast. A car had hooted at him farther back and he was off at a kind of gallop. Sort of. I think he turned in that gravel pit down the road. He yours?'

'No, but I'm looking for him. Thanks.'

The gravel pit had steep, sandy sides. She could probably trap the horse there. Dora took off her belt to slip it through the halter, if she could get a hand on him.

The bottom of the gravel pit was overgrown thickly with bushes and brambles. Dora skirted round the edge and then she saw that the horse had gone out at the far end by floundering up a steep slope.

'Come on, Rob!'

Robin, like all good horses, responded to the challenge of a hill. He gathered his powerful quarters under him, and with an enormous bound, propelled himself to the top in a plunging gallop. Dora put her arms round his neck and hung on. She followed the horse's hoof prints along a path through a small beech wood and out on to another road, which ran along the back gardens of houses.

She had come out on the edge of a suburban development. She jogged round the streets for a while, followed by tots on tricycles and little girls running along the pavement crying, 'Can I pat him?'

Three of the girls ran with her for a long way, panting and puffing and gazing at Robin with adoring eyes. At the corner, Dora stopped and let them catch up to pat him. She could remember when she had been a little girl, running to the window any time a horse went past, cutting pictures out of magazines, in love with her uncle's carthorse, dreaming that one day she would live and work with horses.

'Did you see a loose horse?'

One of the girls nodded, stroking Robin's shoulder.

'Which way?'

'Down there.'

'No, down there, stupid!'

'You blind? It was that way.'

The girls began to fight and kick and pull at each other's clothes. Dora rode on, asking people she passed on their way home with shopping bags, 'Did a loose horse go by here?'

Most of them shook their heads and hurried on, but a woman hanging out laundry in her back garden turned and smiled.

'That big fat thing? It gets out once in a while. The fence isn't strong. Headed for home, it was. It always goes home after a bit.'

'Thanks. I won't worry then.'

The woman pegged down a flapping sheet and came over to the fence.

'You from that place,' she jerked her head, 'up in the hills, where they have all those horses?'

'Follyfoot Farm, yes.'

'My brother took some ponies there once. Two little Welsh.'

'Taffy and Coffee. Taffy is lame, but Coffee lives with a boy in the village.'

'Nice little chaps, they were. My brother was ever so pleased.'

The woman beamed, and invited Dora in for a cup of tea. 'And I've just taken some scones out of the oven.'

Dora's stomach responded instantly, reminding her that she had missed lunch. She took Robin into the garden, and hung the reins over his head to the ground. Because of his western training in America, he stood quietly, as if he was tied.

When she came out of the house and started for home, she realized how far the horse chase had taken her. She went home by the roads instead of cross country, so as not to get lost. Walking on hard surfaces, trotting on grass verges, it seemed for ever before she turned into the winding road that climbed the hill to Follyfoot.

Dusk had fallen out of a dull grey sky, much too early, a warning of short winter days, coming all too soon. Robin was not tired. He trotted up the last slope, anxious for his feed, but when Dora slid to the ground in the stable yard, her knees told her how long she had been in the saddle, and she almost sat down.

The horses that stayed in at night were already in their loose boxes, eating hay. Cobbler's Dream, who liked to supervise comings and goings, put his head over the half door and took a nip at Robin to hustle him into his box.

In the feed shed, there was a note in the oat scoop. *'Everybody fed. All gone to cinema.'*

They might have waited. Dora slammed open the feed bin. Here she was, out all day, doing their job for them, and they couldn't even wait for her. She had been right about nothing good happening.

She fed Robin and gave him a small amount of water and hay. She would come back later to turn him out after he had cooled off. She threw the feed bowl back into the bin, kicked the shed door shut behind her and dragged her tired legs into the house to take it out on Anna for letting the others go off without her.

Everybody was gone, even Anna and the Colonel. Another note on the stove said, 'Your lunch in warming oven. Late supper when we come back.'

Dora sat down to eat the plate of lunch, feeling very lonely and unwanted. This is how she would feel if she were sacked from Follyfoot. Perhaps they were trying to prepare her.

8

WITH the coming of darkness, a breeze got up, and the door of
the feed shed, which had not latched when Dora kicked it
shut, blew open.

Cobbler's Dream observed this glimpse of the open door of
heaven from across the yard, and began to work on the top
bolt of his door.

He was the cleverest horse in the stable. With his muscular,
rubbery lips, designed to work their way round a tuft of grass
to prepare it for cropping by strong teeth, he could sometimes
jiggle and fiddle the bolt and get his door open.

It so happened that Steve had oiled the bolts this week. Very
obliging of him. The bolt slid back, and the Cobbler pushed
the door open with his knee. He strolled across the yard,
shouldered his way into the feed shed, and dragged down a
hundredweight sack of horse nuts which was propped against
the wall.

The sack was sewn across the top, but he tore a hole in it
with his teeth, and with a contented sigh, began to eat.

Dora had gone to sleep in the bath. When her chin slid under
water, she woke spluttering, got out, pulled on some clothes
and went outside again to put Robin out for the night.

Half way down the buildings on one side of the yard, a bulk
was sticking out of an open doorway. It was the back end of
Cobbler's Dream. The front end was still eating.

He was going slow at this point, just messing the food about,
pawing at the sack and spilling horse nuts over the floor.

Dora pulled him out by the tail, scolded him and shut the door. He was liable to bouts of colic, this pony, and although he seemed all right, Dora checked him for signs of trouble – distended stomach, tight skin, distressed eye.

She put a headcollar on him and walked him round the yard for a while before she put him in his box with a rug on him. When she came back after turning Robin out, Cobby seemed comfortable, but Dora stayed with him for a while to make sure he did not lie down and risk twisting intestines that might become filled with gas after over-eating.

Two hours later, when Dora was asleep in one corner of the straw and the chestnut pony was dozing in the other, resting a hind leg, lashes drooping over a bleary eye, the door opened and Callie came in.

'You missed a super film.'

She began to tell Dora the plot even before she came awake. 'It was about this man who had a thing for climbing up the outsides of skyscrapers, and there was this other man behind a window on the forty-eighth – no, the forty-seventh floor, and he was trapped there because he knew something about this other man – not the one who was climbing up the sky-scraper, but the one who'd killed the man who – what's the matter with Cobby? Is he all right?'

'Doesn't deserve to be.' Dora was awake blinking in the light from Callie's torch. 'He got into the feed shed.'

'How?'

'I left the door open.'

'Oh.' Callie switched off the torch. She knew how Dora would feel. There was no need to discuss that. 'Steve and Ron went to a dance place after the film,' she said. 'I came home with Mum and the Colonel.' Callie's mother was married to the

Colonel, which made him her stepfather, but she called him the Colonel, because everybody else did. 'You're to come in for supper.'

'I don't want any. I'll stay here for a while. Good night, Cal.'

'I haven't gone yet.'

Callie went over to put an arm round Cobby's neck, mingling her long brown hair with his chestnut mane.

'Dora,' she said, not looking at her, 'what was the meeting about this morning, with you and the others?'

'Oh – about money, of course. Everything horrid always is.'

'I'm sick of money. That's all we hear at school. All those rotten maths problems are about money. I'm fed up with it.'

'So am I,' said Dora, 'but it does buy oats and things, and pay the blacksmith. And us. Now there's not enough to pay us.'

'Why don't you work for nothing?'

'The Colonel won't let me. He's in a difficult mood. The Trustees have been bothering him. They told him one of us would have to go.'

'That's stupid.' Callie turned round and leaned against Cobby's shoulder. 'There's too much work as it is. Who'd go anyway?'

'Not me,' Dora said. 'I couldn't.'

'No,' Callie said, 'because then you'd have to grow up and be like other people.'

'Aren't I grown up?'

'Not really.'

'Good.' It was Dora's birthday tomorrow. No one had remembered, and she was not going to tell them.

'And Steve couldn't go,' Callie said. 'Who'd lift bales

31

and things, and drive the horse box? And Ron.' She gave a short laugh. 'Poor old Ron. Who else would have him? Slugger can't do much work, but the Colonel would never kick him out, any more than he'd kick out one of the old horses.'

9

IN his cottage across the road, Slugger lay in the sagging brass bed with the patchwork quilt his wife had made before her fingers stiffened and her eyes grew weak.

Slugger had been on his own in the cottage for five years, since his wife died. The Colonel and Anna had wanted him to move across the road into the farm house, but the cottage was his shell, a container of the memories of all the years since he had been with the Colonel at Follyfoot.

Slugger's daughter had grown up and married from this cottage. All the things of his life were crammed into the tiny rooms with the low ceilings and sprigged wallpaper. The furniture he and Nellie had collected, the china souvenirs of their holidays, the pictures of Helen's wedding and the pictures of her sons and the pictures and pictures and pictures of all the horses Slugger had ever known.

He had gone to bed early, bumping his head six times on the pillow, which was safer and less aggravating than an alarm clock, and then thumping it once more for something very important he had to remember tomorrow.

He slept for what seemed like hours, then woke suddenly and put out an arm across the bed – stupid old fool, Nellie hadn't been there for five years. He tossed and muttered and counted herds of wild ponies, but he could not sleep again.

He got up to get his biscuit tin, and looked out of the window.

It was raining, a warm autumn drizzle that would keep the leaves from dying and falling too soon. Through a gap between buildings across the road, he saw a small light moving in the yard. Someone gone out to check the horses. Dora probably, good girl that she was. Or Steve. Slugger smiled when he thought of how much Steve had changed since he came, a prickly, silent boy, who had grown strong and dependable.

It was a good life here. How could Slugger bear to leave? He couldn't, of course, and the Colonel would never sack him. Hadn't they sworn, that night in the bomb shelter, to stick together, if they ever got out alive? But if someone had to go, Slugger was the obvious one, since he could no longer do his share of the work.

'But I'll not go,' he said to the invisible Nellie, with whom he still exchanged ideas.

You'll have to go, old man, she replied in her practical fashion, *if it's to help the Colonel.*

With his teeth out, Slugger mumbled on the softened biscuit. He wandered round the room, touching things and stumbling over the dog.

For pity's sake, Nellie admonished inside his head, *you've got something important to do in the morning. Get back into bed and go to sleep.*

'All right, all right.' Slugger climbed into the bed, turned over on his side away from the memory of Nellie, and was asleep.

When he woke promptly at six the next morning, he could not remember what he had thought about in the night, nor what it was he had to remember. Something only he knew about. Yes – that was it. He sat up and threw off the quilt. Dora's birthday. Nobody else had remembered, not even Dora. She blanked out birthdays, since she was dead set against growing up.

·   ·   ·   ·   ·

There was no telephone in Slugger's cottage. He had to wait until the farm house was empty, to make his important secret call.

Half way through the morning, Callie was at school, Dora and Steve and Ron out working, and Anna had taken the Colonel to the doctor.

Slugger went into the Colonel's study, and sat down at the desk, frowning at the telephone. He looked up the number of the cake shop, and cautiously dialled it with his shaky, knotted fingers.

It took him three tries before the call went through.

'Prudence's Cake Shop.' The woman sounded flustered and hot, as if she had just come from the ovens, and was getting flour all over the telephone.

'I want to order a birthday cake,' Slugger said, 'to pick up this afternoon.' He would make an excuse to take the truck and sneak into town, so he could surprise Dora and everyone with the cake at supper.

It took quite a time to settle on the size and colour and flavour, because Slugger kept changing his mind over such important decisions.

'Do you want somebody's name on it?' Prudence sounded impatient.

'I do.' Slugger had thought about that. He did not want an ordinary Happy Birthday message. 'I want "Horsey Birthday, Dora".'

'Happy Birthday, Nora. Got it.'

'No!' shouted Slugger. 'Dora. D as in dinner.'

'Happy Birthday, Dora.'

'Don't muck about. It's Horsey Birthday. Horsey, see?'

'Naughty?' You could hear the woman raising her floury eyebrows. 'Naughty Birthday? I don't believe that Prudence's Cake Shop – I mean, we do have a reputation to maintain.'

'Belt up, woman and listen.' Slugger was desperate. 'I'm paying for this cake, see, and I want Horsey Birthday, Dora and the picture of a horse's head on it – a thoroughbred, mind – in pink icing.'

He was so worn out by this tiresome conversation that he had to go and lie down for a while on the Colonel's lumpy, dog-haired couch.

10

THE grey blur of rain had lifted. It was a glorious Indian summer day, the sky deep blue, the sun as strong as summer.

Something must be done to celebrate the season. An autumn ride would be the thing. They would invite all the local people with horses and ponies and take a long ride through the woods and stubble fields together, before the bad weather set in and it was too late.

Dora and Steve and Ron lay on their stomachs on the patch of grass by the barn, with an ordnance map spread out on the ground, planning the ride. Through the big wood and along the ridge, across the dip between Mark's Hill and the Bump down into the hollow by the dairy farm. They would have to make a detour here, as they could not cross the main road with a crowd of kids on ponies. Through Marston village with a stop for lunch on the common, and across the canal to the old tow path.

'We can't go across the road bridge, with all that traffic,' Steve said. 'We could sneak over the footbridge at the end of the valley, if we could go through Carter's coal yard. Would he let us?'

'He'd probably shoot us,' Dora said. 'Last time I tried to go through there, he set his dogs on me.'

'Yeah, he would.' Mr Carter was one of Ron's doubtful acquaintances, someone he kept on the right side of.

'Can you ask him, Ron, whether we can go through with a crowd of kids? He doesn't like horses, does he?'

'Or kids.'

Mr Carter did not like anything that had no profit for him.

37

'Are you scared to ask him?'

'Knock it off. Do anything for me, Mr Carter would. "Just name it, Ron," he says.'

'All right, name that we want him to let a funny looking crowd of people on unfit horses and hairy ponies through his coal yard and over the footbridge.'

'He'll let *me* through,' Ron said grandly. 'The hairy mob will follow. I better not get sacked before the ride.'

'What are you plotting?' The Colonel came out of the barn, where he had been looking over the winter's store of hay.

'An autumn ride,' Dora sat up. 'Going to come with us? Stroller's quite sound.' The Colonel sometimes rode the old brewery horse.

'How far are you going?'

'About ten miles.'

'Bit far for Stroller,' the Colonel said. But he really meant, *a bit far for me*.

'I say, Col.' As the Colonel turned to walk away, Ron rolled over and squinted up at him. 'You didn't really mean that, did you, what you said at the business meeting?'

The Colonel stopped and turned round. 'Yes,' he said, staring with no expression over the tops of the apple trees. 'Yes, I'm afraid I did.' He turned again and went towards the house.

As they got up from the grass, they saw Slugger, who had come across the road from his cottage and was climbing with some difficulty into the cab of the small truck.

'Where are you going?' Steve called. Slugger hardly ever drove.

'Into town.' Slugger stopped with one foot in the cab of the truck and one on the step. 'Got some things to get.'

'I'll drive you,' Dora said.

'That's all right.' Slugger seemed a bit flustered. 'I'll manage.'
He got in and shut the door.

'You look very suspicious.' Dora went up to the window.
'Have you got a date with a girl?'

'Course he has,' Ron said. 'Going to a tea dance, innee?'

'That's it,' Slugger grinned. 'That's why I got me teeth in.'

'Are you sure you need to go?' Steve asked. 'I've got to do
some shopping tomorrow. I could get your stuff.'

Slugger's driving was awful. They always tried to find
excuses not to let him use the truck.

'If it's all right with you, boss,' Slugger looked down at him,
'I'll go today.'

'I don't care. Just be sure and put some petrol in the truck.
It's almost empty.'

'I know that,' Slugger said, although he had actually forgotten
to look at the petrol gauge. 'I'm not blind.'

'Hang on a minute,' Dora said. 'I'll get Folly's headcollar. It's
got to be taken to the tack shop to be mended.'

Ron fished in his pocket and brought out a broken guitar
string. 'As long as you're going to the shops, you might go to
that music place, Sight and Sound, they call it, and get me
another one of these.'

Dora came back with the broken headcollar which had been
tied with string, and threw it on the seat of the truck. Slugger
started the engine on the fifth try, crashed into gear, moved
forward in a series of jerks, and almost ran into Anna, turning
into the gateway in her car.

She got out and came to the truck window. 'Where are you
going?'

'To the shops.' He clutched the wheel grimly. He'd never
get away.

'Oh good.' She took a ticket out of her coat pocket. 'You
can fetch my skirt at the cleaner's.'

39

As he took the ticket and the money she gave him, Slugger saw Callie walking from the bus stop with her school bag. Before she could burden him with another errand, he rolled up his window and made a fast getaway, kicking up the gravel and sounding his horn at a stone by the roadside that he thought was a cat.

II

SLUGGER negotiated the steep winding hill below Follyfoot with great care, as if he were coming down a mountain road in Switzerland. Once on to the straight road at the bottom, he settled down to his usual steady pace. At thirty-five miles an hour in the middle of the road, he drove serenely along, singing 'Born Free' in a cracked tenor, with four or five cars behind him, hooting and flashing their lights.

To their relief, he turned the truck into a side road, to take his favourite short cut into town. It was actually longer in distance and in time, but it got him away from traffic and into the country lanes he enjoyed.

He changed his song to one of the more solemn ones with which he expressed contentment. 'Abide with me' was quite nice to drive to. The autumn woods were changing to brown and red, with flares of yellow in the clear light. A whole population of migrating birds circled in a corner of the sky, forming up for their long journey.

This was a familiar road to Slugger. He checked off the landmarks as he came to them. The tree split by lightning. The hedge where he saw the two badgers. The church where his niece Ada had married that fellow nobody liked. The Bunkers' house where they had the fire in the stable and Jim's pony Barney had bitten off the tip of Mrs Bunker's finger, in the days before Dora made a Christian of him.

Mrs Bunker was out in the garden with a basket and a big hat with a scarf round it, cutting dahlias. Farther on, Slugger passed the field where Barney had been turned out to grass when Jim went away to school.

The bay pony was grazing near the gate. Slugger gave him a hoot and a friendly salute, in memory of the night when he had won the Moonlight Steeplechase against all those fancy ponies, and Slugger had nearly had a heart attack from excitement.

A little farther on, the truck began to falter and cough. Dratted thing. Slugger never could come to terms with engines. He pressed down on the accelerator, but nothing happened. The truck stopped. Failing to start it again, he switched off the engine, looked out of the window for two minutes, then tried to catch it by surprise. Nothing happened. He tried the starter a few more times, then got out to lift up the bonnet and peer underneath, as if he knew what he expected to find. Everything seemed to be there. He walked round the truck, kicking at the tyres, and even slapped it on the rump, as if it were a stubborn horse.

He got back into the cab, switched on the lights and the turning signals and pushed the heater lever back and forth, then sat back despondently. He looked down at the broken headcollar and the guitar string and Anna's cleaner's ticket – what did they think he was, a common carrier? It was a wonder Steve had not dumped something on him too.

But he had. What was it he had asked? Oh yes. 'Be sure and put some petrol in it.' Slugger had turned off on his favourite short cut before he got to the petrol station.

He switched on the engine and looked at the gauge. The needle did not flicker. Out of petrol.

Slugger got out of the truck and looked up and down the road. Not a soul in sight. The nearest house was the Bunkers.' He would have to walk back and telephone. It was almost a mile. Much too far for his old legs.

He looked at his watch. After four. He must get to the cake

42

shop in time, or there would be no birthday party for Dora this evening.

He looked again up and down the empty road. Barney had his large rather common head hung over the gate of the field, and was observing him mildly.

Slugger called to him, and the pony let out one of his deep, rumbling whinnies, with which he used to greet Slugger coming with food, when he was living at Follyfoot.

Slugger knew what he had to do. He took the headcollar off the seat, and found a length of frayed rope in the back of the truck.

He talked about his riding days in the Army, because the Colonel had been in the Cavalry, but in actual fact, he had hardly ridden at all. At Follyfoot, the Colonel and Steve and Dora and Callie and even Ron had tried to persuade him to ride, but although he was fond of the horses and enjoyed taking care of them, he remained firmly on the ground.

But this was an emergency. He opened the gate of the field and went inside. The pony came to him, and after some difficulty with the string, Slugger got the broken headcollar on and fixed the piece of rope to it.

He brought the pony out, climbed up two rails of the gate and put one leg over Barney's back. Thank God he was only a little 'un. There was a moment of suspense while Slugger hung between the pony and the gate. If the pony had moved, it would have been all up. The pony stood by the gate and Slugger managed to wriggle on board.

'Home, James!' Slugger hauled his head round and got him started down the road towards the house, hanging on to the mane and feeling very weak and insecure.

The pony was fat and slippery. When he jogged, Slugger flopped helplessly from side to side. If this was the riding the kids were so daft about, they could have it. Dora's birthday cake. He set his jaw and hung on.

It would have been all right, if a motorbike had not come down a track between the fields and suddenly shot out into the road right in front of Barney's nose.

The pony shied drastically away, and Slugger pitched forward over his head with his hands flung out to try and save himself.

A jar like the cracking of a fault in the earth's crust ran up one arm to his shoulder. Then his head hit the road and exploded in a white flash that carried with it all the photographs in his cottage of weddings and children and Nellie and horses and horses and horses, as he reeled out of the world.

12

MRS Bunker's dahlias had not done very well this year. There were not many flowers to cut. Most of the dahlias had been eaten away by bees, slugs, and the various unspeakable insects that seemed to wage a private war against Mrs Bunker's garden.

She had to content herself with cutting off dead and riddled dahlias and throwing them on the compost heap by the stable. She added a shovel of manure, as the gardening books told you to do. That was one thing, at least, she knew that horses were good for. She had not learned much else beyond the truth that they were dangerous at both ends and uncomfortable in the middle. She glanced at the tip of her shortened finger, as she always did when she thought about horses.

She was turning to go into the house to start preparing dinner for Mr Bunker, when she heard a wild clatter of hoofs in the road. Jim's pony dashed into the drive and came to a dead stop on the Bunkers' lawn, tearing at the short grass as if he had not eaten for months.

'Barney! You wicked thing. You're supposed to be in that lovely field down the road. Have you broken a fence again, you bad, bad creature?'

She shook her fist at him. Barney walked over the corner of the chrysanthemum bed to get to a patch of clover. There was no one to help her. Her husband would not be home for two hours.

Courage, Marion Bunker. She went into the tool shed where the oats were kept, put some in a bowl and walked cautiously over the lawn to shake it in front of the pony's nose, at arm's length, standing well away from him. As he reached for it, she retreated, trying to lure him towards the stable.

Walking backwards to keep an eye on him, she stumbled against the wheelbarrow, tore her nylons on a bush, and turned her ankle on a stone, but she managed to get him to follow her to the door of the loose box, where she shoved the bowl inside, and shut the door on him as he went in after the oats.

'You stay there, you wretched creature.' She wagged the mutilated finger at him. 'I'm going up to see where you got out, and if there's much damage done, you'll pay for it, you mark my words, when Mr Bunker gets home.'

In her red minibus, which had a plastic flower fixed to the top of the aerial, she drove down the road to the field. If the gate was open, she would know that it was those bad boys from the village, up to their tricks again. When she rounded the corner, she saw that the gate was shut. So it was not bad boys, but bad Barney, breaking fences again.

Near the gate, she saw what looked like a heap of clothes lying at the side of the road. What an extraordinary place –

She slowed, then stopped, and got out quickly. It was not a heap of clothes, it was a person. It was an unconscious person. It was that old man from Follyfoot Farm, lying on his side in a crumpled way, one arm flung out as if reaching for help, the other bent under him in an odd, unnatural way.

As Mrs Bunker stopped to lift him, the old man opened his eyes with a yell.

'What's happened?'

He groaned and shut his eyes again.

It had been a task for Mrs Bunker to get Barney into the stable, but that was nothing compared to getting the old man into the minibus.

'Come on, you can't lie here.'

She got her arm under what seemed to be his good shoulder and sat him up, leaning against her. She took the scarf from her hat and made a sling to support what was obviously a broken arm. When she managed to get the man on to his feet, he fainted, but she was able to prop him up, since he was very light. Half dragging, half carrying him, she got him into the bus. He lay back in the seat, pale as paper, and she was afraid that he would die before they got to the hospital, of old age, if nothing else.

13

WHEN Slugger was let out of the hospital, walking with a sideways tilt, partly because of the heavy plaster cast from wrist to shoulder, partly because he was still groggy, Anna would not let him stay alone in his cottage. She insisted that he sleep in the spare room at the Farm.

It was the best room in the house. Anna kept the door locked, so the cats could not go in and take over the bed, and people could not wander in to dump bits of the debris that silted up their own bedrooms.

Dora's room was an inferno of last winter's sweaters still waiting to be washed, horse pictures, plans for the new stable block they were going to build if they ever got the money, horse books and magazines, some ears of dried oats and bull-rushes sticking out of the tall silver cup she and Barney had won in the Moonlight Steeplechase.

Callie's room, you could not get into. Not because it was more untidy than Dora's, but because she had fixed a kind of gate across the door to make it into a stable. With more than twenty horses outside, she still spent a large part of her time being a horse herself.

No good redecorating those rooms, so Anna had let herself go in the spare room, with white paint, flower-splashed wall-paper, pink sheets and new chintz curtains and bedspread.

When Callie took in Slugger's breakfast, he was sitting up in the bed like a little old gnome in striped pyjamas, his weathered face and work-worn hands dark against the pink frilled pillow-case and sheets.

'You do look posh.' Callie put down the tray, and stroked the silky eiderdown.

'Don't I?' Slugger snuggled his head against the pillow. 'Worth breaking me arm any day of the week.'

Callie went to the window to draw the curtains, which filtered a pink light through the room, as if Slugger was living in a bowl of strawberry ice. Outside, a touch of night frost had left the lawn sparkling with a thousand crystals. Perfect day to ride. She began to invent possible excuses for not going to school.

Behind her, she heard the Colonel come into the room.

'Morning, Slugger.'

'Morning, Colonel.'

'Well then.'

'Well then.'

They knew each other so well, they communicated in a kind of shorthand.

'It looks as if your insurance is coming through,' the Colonel said. 'They'll give you a decent weekly amount until you can start work again.'

'Ah.'

'Yes,' said the Colonel, as if Slugger had spoken a whole sentence. 'That's what I was thinking.'

'Takes care of that then,' Slugger said.

'For a bit.'

'Takes care of what?' Callie turned round when the Colonel had gone.

'I'll get my sick pay, see, so he can tell the Trustees he's saving on one man's wages. Good joke, innit?'

'Not much of a joke,' Callie said, 'if a person has to break their arm to solve a stupid money problem.'

'That's the way it is though, girl.' Slugger shoved the tray down to the bottom of the bed, and nestled down again into the pink sheets. A cat that had been under the eiderdown came out and began to clean off the plate. 'When you got an unsolvable problem, it takes some daft beggar like old Barney to find the answer.'

14

THE immediate danger was over. They could breathe again. They could enjoy the autumn ride without the unspoken threat: this might be the last ride for one of us – which one?

Everybody turned out for the Saturday morning ride. Everybody, that is, who had any kind of a horse or pony that could manage the ten mile distance.

Some of them could only manage it if they took it at their own pace. Dora and Robin spent part of the ride cantering up ahead to tell the competitive girls from the pony farm to slow down, it wasn't a race, and the rest cantering back to round up people like Johnnie Hatch on a low-slung ball of fur called Phoebe, who went all the way at an even jiggle, with no saddle on her broad back, and no bridle on her wooly head. There was no point in putting a bit in Phoebe's mouth. She just followed the other horses anyway.

It was a glorious day, with the ground neither too frozen nor too muddy, and the horses snorting briskly in the crisp air.

They trotted through Marston village, surprising Saturday shoppers, and came out on to the common on the other side to find Anna and some of the other mothers in the truck, with fried chicken and doughnuts and an urn of hot cocoa.

It was almost half an hour before everybody had collected together. The pony farm girls on their New Forests and Dartmoors, Ron on the mule, Toby on his welsh pony Coffee, Mrs Oldcastle on Harold, Callie on Hero, Steve on Cobbler's Dream, Jim Bunker, home for the weekend, on Barney, skinny Alice Hatch on her skinny pony, Dora, last to arrive, leading Phoebe by her halter, with Johnnie on the front of Robin's saddle. It was the only way to get them there before the others ate all the lunch.

When they were ready to start again, Johnnie Hatch was asleep on the seat of the truck. Steve and Ron picked up Phoebe and put her in the back of the truck with the cocoa urn, for Anna to take home.

Having been helped down from Harold to eat her chicken, Mrs Oldcastle needed help to get back on again. Ron gave her a leg-up and heaved so hard, she would have gone right over the other side, if Dora had not been hanging on to the stirrup, and could push her back into the saddle.

'That's better.' Mrs Oldcastle adjusted her hat and picked up her reins as if they were a conductor's baton. 'Thank you, young man.' She never knew anybody's name. 'I know you, don't I? You were in my house. I gave you a carroway cake.'

'Chocolate.' Ron looked up at her under the curled brim of his cowboy hat. 'And you threw me out.'

'Because you let your horse into my vegetable garden.'

'No, because I asked you for help, and you –'

'Well, there'll be no more stray horses in my carrots and sprouts, I can tell you that.' Mrs Oldcastle tapped him on the hat with her whip, like the Queen conferring a knighthood. 'I bought an airgun and pellets and I'm not afraid to use it, young man, remember that.'

Ron ducked as the whip lifted again, and she rode off calling, 'Come along, everybody I'm tired of waiting!' although everybody had been waiting for *her*.

They pounded off down the broad turfy stretch in the middle of the common, and all jumped together over the small ditch at the end.

Not all together. Dora turned and saw that two of the ponies had refused, Alice Hatch had fallen off and was looking for her glasses, and Willie the mule was on the wrong side of the ditch, leaning back with heels dug in, while Ron had his heels dug in on the other side, tugging at the reins.

Dora jumped Robin back again, picked a stick, and shooed the refusing ponies over. Willie would not budge. Ron stepped back across the ditch, vaulted into the old Army saddle and said he was going home.

'We can't go through the coal yard without you.'

'You'll have to go by the road.'

'There's too much traffic. Ron, you must. Make him jump. Get up, you, Willie!'

She whacked at the mule's stringy grey quarters with the stick, and broke it. Ron sat there, kicking with his cowboy boots, and the mule sighed and put his head down to eat the coarse grass at the edge of the ditch.

'Come on!' Steve shouted. The others were tired of waiting. Mrs Oldcastle's nose was going blue. Alice Hatch's pony was out of control, because her glasses were broken and she could not see.

'I'll make him.' Dora got off Robin, pulled Ron off the mule and got on herself. She knew Willie of old. It was she who had taught him to jump, if you could call it jumping.

You had to take him by surprise. She walked him to the edge of the ditch, then turned him sideways, as if they were going to stay on this side. Then she suddenly tugged his head round and gave him a huge kick, and before he knew it, his front end was over, followed after a moment of standing spreadeagled over the ditch, by the unwilling back end.

'Ta.'

Ron stepped over the ditch, Robin hopped over by himself, and they cantered after the others.

The green common deteriorated into wasteland, with a dump of old cars on the edge of the run-down district by the canal.

They went in single file down the alley between the backs of the houses. At the gate of the coal yard, Mr Carter lumbered out of his office, a huge man, too fat to breathe. Ron spoke to him. Mr Carter nodded and wheezed and dropped his rolled chins into the rolled neck of his black sweater. He stood with hands in the pockets of trousers stretched wide over his belly, watching each person come through, as if he would want to know them next time he saw them.

As she rode past the window of a rusted iron shed, Dora thought she saw a face looking out through dirty yellow hair. A face with dark staring eyes that made Dora turn in her saddle to look again.

There was no face. But there was a space rubbed with a finger on the grimy window.

Across the footbridge, they turned thankfully on to the tow-path on the other side of the canal where the land was green again, and the dingy neighbourhood soon left behind. Going from field to field through the narrow gates, they headed for the bottom of the hills, where the canal took a turn, and they could cross it by the humpback bridge and scramble up through the steep path slippery with wet leaves, big birds squalling up out of the trees ahead of them.

At the crossroads, they separated to go their various ways. Dora and Steve and Ron and Callie walked the last stretch of road that Dora loved, because it led to home, and went past one of their fields. Nigger and Frank and stiff old Ginger trotted up to the gate and called a welcome.

Through the lighted window of his study, she saw the Colonel stand up when he heard the hoofs in the road, and reach for his jacket on the back of the door. He was out in the yard with the dogs barking round him, as they rode in.

15

THE Colonel had been to the doctor for a medical examination before he went abroad. Since his lung trouble, he and Anna had to go away for a while every winter to give him a healing dose of sun.

Before they left, the Colonel held another staff meeting. Not solemn and frightening, like the one they had had in his study about cutting down staff, but casually, in the hay shed.

He found Steve and Dora bagging chaff, while Callie and Ron played cards on a bale of hay, and Slugger turned the creaking handle of the chaff-cutting machine with his one good arm.

'Well then.' The Colonel picked up a stalk of hay to chew. 'We're off in the morning. You'll be all right then?'

'Of course,' said Dora, 'if we're left alone.'

Once, he had moved in a dreadful woman called Phyllis Weatherby to take charge while he was away. They had got rid of her by fair means and foul. Mostly foul.

'Just remember then.' The Colonel put his hands in his pockets. 'No more horses till I get back.'

'We know that.' Dora thought about poor Ellis Elkins and his horse that was 'sort of a mottled colour', and was probably either dead by now, or going lame in the riding school.

'You've got a full stable,' the Colonel said. 'All you can manage.'

'We'll be all right,' Steve said.

'And so will the horses,' Ron added, 'in case no one's thought of them.'

'None of them is likely to conk out before I get back,' the

Colonel said, 'but you'll have to watch that leg of Ginger's, and if Cobby gets into trouble again, give him a drench without waiting to see how he feels. Dolly's feet are going to need trimming soon, and a few others, and if the Weaver doesn't stop coughing, you'd better isolate him in the foaling stable. Yes, I know.' He gave Dora a look. 'That would mean an empty loose box. Better let it stay empty. No more horses.'

'Does that include ponies?' Callie slapped down a card. 'Gotcher, Ron.'

'And donkeys,' the Colonel added, remembering the time when Dora's American friend Mr Blankenheimer had bought Dottie in the market and driven her here on the back seat of his car.

'So if,' Ron liked to give people a hard time, 'so if some horse come travelling up the road on three legs, waving the fourth and crying, "Save me, I'm dying," we just wave it on and say, "Keep travelling," right?'

'And so if,' said Callie, 'some poor old lady like Mrs Berry turns up at the gate with a home-made trailer and a horse that was doomed to be shipped abroad for slaughter, we're just to say, "Sorry, Mrs Berry, we don't take in horses that are doomed to be shipped for slaughter any more."'

'Stop trying to get my goat,' the Colonel said. 'I'm not talking about emergencies. You know what I mean. Do your jobs. I trust you. Any questions?'

'Just one,' Steve said innocently. 'Who's in charge this time?'

When the Colonel was away, Dora was apt to get a bit bossy.

'Yes,' said Dora. 'I'd like to know too.'

When the Colonel was away, Steve was inclined to get a bit bossy.

The Colonel looked at them both and smiled. 'Slugger's in charge. He can supervise.'

'Me?' Slugger patted the heavy cast on his arm. 'Can't even pick up a manure shovel.'

'The supervisor doesn't have to shovel,' the Colonel said. 'That's why you're in charge.'

Slugger shrugged his good shoulder. 'Always was, really.'

16

WHILE Anna was away, they shared her domestic jobs. Slugger could do most of the cooking, if someone helped him with things like peeling and chopping and opening tins, that needed two hands. Callie did the laundry by taking it into the bath with her, and sloshing it round in suds with her hands and feet before putting it through the wringer and hanging it on the line. It was everyone's job to do housework, which meant it was no one's. They would have a massive clean-up the day before Anna came back.

Dora did most of the food shopping. Coming out of the butcher's one day with a bag of sausages and stewing meat and some bones she had begged for the dogs, she almost bumped into a man in a raincoat, walking fast along the pavement with his shoulders hunched.

He side-stepped without raising his eyes and went on, and then he turned back just as Dora turned back and they both said, 'Hullo.'

Having said, 'Hullo', they each had no idea who the other one was.

'Excuse me,' the man said. 'I made a mistake.' He turned to walk on, and the droop of his shoulders reminded Dora.

'Mr Elkins.'

He turned back. 'Yes, and you're –'

'Dora. From Follyfoot Farm.'

'Oh yes.' He nodded curtly, and walked on.

Dora went after him. 'I felt terrible about – you know – not taking the horse.'

'It's all right.' He walked ahead without looking at her.

'What – I mean – what happened to him? Did you –'

'I don't want to talk about it.'

But there was traffic at the crossing, and he had to stop and wait for the lights to change.

'Please tell me.'

Dora had two heavy shopping bags, and although he did not really want to talk, Ellis Elkins was too polite not to take one from her.

'I've been worried about Kingfisher. Did you sell him to the riding school, or did you have to – have to – you know – have him – er, you know?'

Dora had lived with animals long enough to be able to talk sensibly about death, but with Elkins looking so dejected, she could not come out with it.

'I wasn't able to do either of those things.' He turned his creased face and bloodhound eyes to her. 'I'm leaving for South America tomorrow.'

'What are you going to do with him?'

'Nothing *to* do. I thought I'd just turn him loose to wander and fend for himself. It seems kinder. There's grass everywhere, and ponds and things . . .'

'You can't do that! Look – we'll have to take him.'

'But the man in charge at your farm said –'

'The Colonel isn't there at the moment,' Dora said. 'Actually.'

'Who's running it then?'

'I am. Actually. Please, please, *please*, don't turn Kingfisher loose.'

'Well, as a matter of fact,' Ellis Elkins looked at his shabby shoes, 'I did. The day after I came to your place. Actually.'

'Oh, you –' Dora could have slapped him. 'That's terribly dangerous. He could be hit by a car, or caught in wire – anything. You just don't leave horses on their own to wander about.'

'Well, I did.' Ellis Elkins looked at her apologetically. 'Before I shut up my house, I rode King a long way away, where we'd never been before. Then I got off and I put on his best red halter and led him on to some nice grass and said "Farewell".' He blinked. 'Then I threw the saddle and bridle over the wall of a churchyard – like burying your dreams – and got on a bus and went away. Goodbye.'

The lights had been green twice and were now red again, but he stepped off the kerb, and a bicyclist swerved and swore.

'My sausages!'

Dora grabbed her shopping bag, and Elkins weaved away through the traffic like a sleepwalker, and disappeared into the Saturday crowds.

Dora ran back to the car park with the shopping bags bumping against her legs. A fleabitten grey, Mrs Oldcastle had seen in her vegetable garden, and Ellis Elkins had said that Kingfisher was sort of 'mottled and freckled'. If the saddle and bridle were still in the nearby churchyard, then Dora would know for sure.

Reckless with anxiety, she drove the truck as fast as she dared. There was a church at the end of the village beyond the entrance to Mrs Oldcastle's house. Dora whizzed through the village, slowed, and pulled the truck off the road by the wall of the churchyard. She went through the gate and began to look among the graves near the wall.

'Are you looking for a dear departed one?'

A smiling lady in glinting glasses rose from a grave, where she was planting bulbs. 'I know just about everybody here,' she said sociably, as if she were offering to introduce guests at a party.

When Dora told her what she was looking for, the lady beamed.

'Quite a nice saddle it was,' she said. 'German made, but we must face the fact that the British don't have a monopoly on leather goods. We sold it as treasure trove. Just in time to pay the electricity bill. "Saddles from heaven," I said to the vicar. "The Lord will provide."'

Dora hoped that the Lord would provide her with a sight of the fleabitten grey. It must have been Kingfisher she had chased across country that day. Red halter, the digging man had said, and the tea and scones woman had said that the horse was going home. That must be where Elkins used to live.

The tea and scones woman was glad to see her.

'I've just put the kettle on,' she said, 'and there's yesterday's buns.'

But Dora could only stay to find out on which road Ellis Elkins and the horse had lived.

The house was locked up tightly, with the blinds drawn, and a week's supply of wet newspapers rotting on the step. In the back garden, a makeshift stable and a patched up fence round a bare trodden patch looked like a hopeless place to keep a horse.

The window of the stable was boarded up, and a bar of wood nailed across the door. Outside, the ground was heavily trampled, as if the horse had come back and stamped about, trying to get in.

Poor old Kingfisher. Abandoned. Somehow getting himself home, and then finding it locked and barred against him. Dora could imagine him, with his new red halter on his mottled head, turning sadly away.

Where would he turn to?

She asked some of the neighbours, but nobody knew or cared. They had not liked the horse being there. Had complained to the Council many times about the smell. About the flies. Had not seen the horse come back. Did not know Mr

Elkins had gone for good. Close-mouthed, he was, not friendly, and they were not ones to poke their noses into other people's affairs, not they, although they could, if they chose, tell Dora a tale or two about bill collectors, empty gin bottles, runaway wives, etc. etc. etc.

It seemed hopeless. Dora drove round the suburban streets for a while, asking other people, but nobody had seen anything of Kingfisher.

She felt sad-hearted and heavy with failure as she drove home more slowly.

'I feel rotten.'

She found Steve doing accounts at the Colonel's desk, and flopped down on the hearthrug to tell him about it.

'I know.' Steve swivelled the chair round to look at her. 'The horse isn't your responsibility, *but –*'

'Nor is that stupid Elkins, *but –*'

'I know that feeling.' Steve looked down at her wisely, like the Colonel. 'You feel you've let them down.'

Dora nodded, picking at the fringe of the rug that the cats were fraying away, bit by bit, year by year.

'Let's hope he was caught and taken in somewhere. Have you rung up the Cruelty to Animals people?'

'Yes, and the police. No news. I told them we could take him here, if they –'

'The Colonel already told the man No.'

'But this is an emergency!' Dora sat up.

'Don't shout at me. Slugger's in charge.'

'Who takes my name in vain?' Slugger looked in from the passage.

'A person's horse is loose,' Dora said. 'He turned it loose, and then went away. If it's found, we have to take it in.'

'I don't think so.' Slugger shook his grey head.

'But it's an emergency.'
'Not yet. Not till they find him.'

Two days later, Dora got a telephone call from the police. A grey horse had been hit by a car at night, at a place where the road ran through open moorland. The driver broke two ribs on the steering wheel and cut his head on the rear view mirror.

'But the horse?' Dora's throat was tight. 'What happened to the horse?'

'Two legs broken. Had to be put down. I'm sorry, Miss. Was it yours?'

'Not exactly.'

But when she hung up the receiver, Dora felt just as bad as if he had been hers, this poor old horse she had never laid eyes on.

17

DORA went out through the kitchen. Slugger was kneading bread dough.

'Don't worry,' she said. 'That grey horse won't be coming.'

'Eh?' Slugger raised his head, the stubby fingers of his good hand pushing and pummelling at the rubbery dough.

Dora tugged open the back door and went out.

Before she talked to anybody, she had to go off on her own for a while to battle with her emotions. She did not want to weep when she talked about Kingfisher. Follyfoot was a place for courage, not sentiment.

Robin was out in the sun, thoughtfully eating bark off a young tree. Dora made a mental memo to tack wire netting round the tree trunk. She put on the saddle and bridle, which she had brought out so that no one would see her leave, and rode out of the hill pasture by the lower gate that led to the edge of the moor.

She rode for a long time, thinking about nothing, as you can when you are on a good horse and can abandon yourself to the pure pleasure of the rhythm and power, the shoulder muscles moving smoothly by your knee, hoofs reaching forward, pounding the turf, tucked up to reach strongly forward again, the finest view in the world the one framed by a pair of inward-curving ears.

But when she pulled Robin to a walk up a stony track, all the thoughts came back again. It wasn't the Colonel's fault. It was hers. If she had stayed to beg or insist, instead of going sulkily out of the tack room, he would have agreed to take the horse in. If she had not stopped for tea and scones with the

64

Welsh pony man's sister, if she had looked further round the streets, she might have found Kingfisher near his home. The horse was dead, from stupidity. She had been just as stupid as Ellis Elkins.

Grief is usually one quarter unselfish sorrow for the dead, and three quarters selfish regret. If only . . . if only . . .

Dora, who usually made Robin either walk, or trot out, let him jog restlessly along the edge of the sticky ploughland at the upper edge of the wood. His head was up, his ears tensely forward.

'What's the matter?' Dora put a hand on his neck. He whinnied, and lengthened the jog to a trot, and as they rounded a corner, there was a girl on a brown pony, riding bareback, with her shoulders hunched in a boy's duffle coat, and tangled yellow hair falling over her face.

The pony stopped and turned round. The girl flapped the reins on its neck, but it stood still. As Dora approached she saw that she did not know either the girl or the pony, which was odd, since she knew all the people who owned horses for miles round.

'Have you come a long way?'

The girl nodded, without raising her head, and muttered, 'I got lost.'

'Where are you headed for?'

'That place where they – I don't know – a farm, or something.' She spoke roughly, mumbling through her hair. 'Where they rescue horses.'

'Follyfoot?'

'Mm.' The girl looked sideways up at her, then down again. 'That's it. I been riding all day. I'm lost.'

'Not now. That's where I live. Come on, I'll take you there.'

The girl would not answer any questions. She trailed along behind Dora, flopping when the pony jogged, like a doll losing

65

its stuffing. The only thing she said was an occasional, 'How much farther?' in an exhausted croak. When they finally came to the pasture gate, Dora got off to open it, because the latch was stiff. The girl swayed as the pony went through, and Dora grabbed her arm.

'Hang on,' she said. 'Almost there.'

In the yard, she got off Robin just in time to catch the girl as she slid off the pony, crumpled, and blacked out.

Dora shouted for help, but there was no one about. The pony and Robin, both loose, began to introduce themselves by squealing and striking out. Dora had to lay the girl down on the cobbles and grab them both. She put Robin in his box and tied the pony to a ring in the wall.

Although its rider looked so wretched and scruffy, it was rather a nice brown pony, well made with a small, intelligent head, trimmed and shod, as if it was well cared for.

As Dora turned back to the girl, she saw that her eyes were open.

'Are you all right?' she asked. 'Who are you? What's the matter?'

For answer, the girl closed her eyes again. She was quite small, not much bigger than Callie. She lay on the cobbles like a child asleep, head on one arm, her pale tousled hair covering her dirty face.

Dora was bending to pick her up, when she remembered you were not supposed to touch a body until you knew where it was hurt. She left her there and ran into the house.

Slugger was in the kitchen, ironing. He would not use Anna's electric iron, which gave off blue sparks when you dropped it. He preferred to heat the heavy doorstop flat iron on the stove, and bang away at tablecloths and pillowcases with his good arm, leaving rusty iron outlines when he banged too hard.

66

Dora gabbled her story. 'Come quick, she may be dying of an internal injury!'

The old man carefully set the iron on end at the back of the stove, folded the tablecloth up so the cats would not pull it down, and put on his woollen hat with maddening slowness.

'Quick, Slugger!'

'Can't go out without me shoes then, can I?'

He bent to look under the dresser, but Dora pulled him out of the door in his slippers and hustled him, complaining, out to the yard where the girl was still lying in the same position, like a limp doll flung down.

Slugger, who had some dim first aid memories from the war, poked her in different places, pulled back one eyelid, then stroked the tangled hair back from her bony little face.

'Don't seem nothing wrong,' he said. 'Exhausted, I daresay. How far have you come, girl?' He slapped her cheek gently and raised his voice. 'Who are you?'

She opened one eye and looked at him. The sun was low, and in the slanting light which sent a deep shadow across her face, she looked not like a child any more.

'Who are you?' Slugger asked again, and she groaned and said, 'Where am I?'

'At Follyfoot.' Dora was squatting on the other side of her. 'You wanted to come here, don't you remember?'

The girl shook her head, rolling it back and forth on the cobbles. 'Like a dream . . .'

'Dream or not,' Slugger said briskly, 'she can't lay here. Pick her up, Dora and bring her in the house, and I'll get some tea brewed. Never a dull moment . . .' He ambled towards the kitchen in his slippers to the tune of the automatic grumble with which he greeted any new situation. 'No peace for the wicked . . . something new every day . . .'

As Dora bent to try to pick up the small girl, who went very limp and heavy and did not help, Steve and Callie came round the barn from the small field, leading the colt Folly in his lungeing tack of roller and side reins and mouthing bit.

'What on earth –' Steve ran forward.

'I found her by Badger's woods. She was coming here with that pony. She's ill or something.' Dora puffed, trying to pick up the inert body.

'Here, I'll take her.' Steve picked up the girl quite easily. She put her arms round his neck and he carried her into the house.

18

SLUGGER was back in his cottage now, so the girl was put to bed in the strawberry ice spare room where he had nursed his broken arm.

'Like a bloomin' hospital,' he said, stumping upstairs with a hot water bottle and an extra blanket.

The pony, who had a growing coat, as if he had been kept out, was turned into the small enclosure with the open shed where Specs and Folly, and later Dottie and her donkey foal, had been separated from the other horses.

Next day, when the girl woke and came down to be revived with sausage and egg and the bread which had turned out to be Slugger's best – light and crusty with big holes to fill with butter – she consented to talk a bit, in a rough accent, which was part cockney, part a sort of country dialect hard to recognize.

'Had to take the pony and split,' she said, looking round the table from under her hair in that trapped, suspicious way. 'Nothing for it.'

When someone asked, 'Why?' she said, 'I got to know. Will you take us in?'

'Strictly speaking,' sitting in the Colonel's place, Slugger put his fingertips together and tried to look In Charge, 'we ain't taking no more 'orses 'ere, nor 'umans neither.'

'It's life or death,' the girl said hoarsely. 'Will you take us or won't you?'

Slugger looked round at his troops.

'I say, no.' Ron had been quite nasty about both the girl and the pony when he turned up that morning. 'We need another horse like we need a hole in the head, let alone another human mouth to feed. I thought we was so poor.'

The girl slid him a look under her hair, and for an instant, Dora thought she had seen her before. Then the girl reached across the table for another slice of bread, tore off the good crisp crust and stuffed it into her mouth, and the illusion of having seen her before was gone.

'Of course they must stay,' she said. How could anyone think otherwise, after the terrible thing that had happened with Ellis Elkins and poor doomed Kingfisher?

'You said it,' Ron said. 'I didn't.'

'Steve?' Slugger pointed at him with the breadknife.

'She'll have to tell her story,' Steve said. 'She'll have to come clean.'

The girl said with her mouth full of bread, 'Not till I know I can trust you.'

It was strange. It seemed as if she was putting Follyfoot on trial, not the other way round.

'Tell us your name then.'

'Are you going to call the police?'

'What for?' Steve asked. 'Are you on the run?'

'No. Yes – no. Well, it's Yasmin.' It seemed a most unlikely name. She added quickly, 'But I don't use it. You can call me Yaz.'

'Yaz what?'

'Just Yaz.'

She was dressed in faded blue jeans, hacked off at the bottom and worn right through at the knees, a man's shirt, violent coloured socks, each one a different colour, and more hole than sock, and frayed grey sneakers. She was rather dirty. Her skin looked as if she had not washed for days. Her dry, straw-coloured hair was cut raggedly, as if she had chopped it herself with a pair of blunt scissors.

She pushed away her plate with a sigh, leaned back in her chair and asked Slugger for a cigarette.

'You're too young.'

'How old do you think I am?'

'Fourteen – fifteen?'

At times she looked even less than that. Sometimes she looked much older.

'I'm twenty.' Yaz clicked her fingers at Ron, who slid a packet of cigarettes across to her.

'All right then.' Slugger leaned forward, resting his plaster cast on the table. 'Let's have your story.'

Yaz lit a cigarette, narrowed her eyes, and looked round at them through the smoke.

'Where did you get the pony?' Steve asked.

'It's mine,' she said defensively.

Dora wanted to say, 'Don't call him it', but she said encouragingly, 'He's a nice pony. Got some New Forest in him, hasn't he?'

'I daresay.'

'Is something wrong with him? He looks fit enough.'

'Well, see, it's like – it's all messed up, you know?'

'No,' said Slugger patiently. 'We don't know. Not till you tell us.'

Yaz looked down at her grubby hands with the black, bitten nails. 'My mother's dead, for a start.' Her small face clouded over. 'I don't want to talk about that. I've been living with my father. He's an artist.'

She stopped. No one said anything. Dora cleared her throat and tried, 'That must be interesting.'

'It's hell.' The girl scowled at her. 'He's a drunk. We live miles away from anywhere, right off in the woods at the end of a muddy old road, with no electricity nor nothing. I do all the work. Look after the house, if you can call it a house.

71

Falling to bits, it is. Cold.' She wrapped her arms round her thin body and shivered. 'Cook for him. Grow the vegetables. Feed those rotten chickens. Clean up the mess when he goes into one of his drunken rages. He hits me sometimes.' She rolled up her sleeve and tilted her face up to the light. She had a bruise on her upper arm and on her right cheek.

'Why do you stay?' Steve asked.

'I promised my mother I'd always look after him.'

She paused. The room was very quiet.

'Why is everyone so quiet?' Callie came bursting in from the stables, mud and manure on her boots, strong wind in her unplaited hair, energy glowing in her face. 'Am I interrupting something?'

'Yaz is telling us her life story.'

'Who's Yaz?'

'This here is Yaz.' Slugger nodded at the girl. 'Take off them boots and shut up.'

'I've been making friends with your pony.' Callie slid into a chair, and grabbed for a piece of bread with one hand and the teapot with the other. 'What's his name?'

Yaz did not seem to hear. 'He's all I've got,' she said, talking as if to herself. 'My mother gave him to me before she died. I've had him for years.'

'He doesn't look all that old.' Callie poured tea and attacked the sugar bowl.

'He's my oldest friend. My only friend. Dad wants to take him away.'

'Why?'

'Because he reminds him of my mother. He wants to have him put down. He was going to send him away to sell him. But I said wherever he went, I'd follow, steal him back, so he said, "All right, I'll shoot him." He would too.'

'It's awful.' Callie was enthralled.

72

'Yesterday – day before – I dunno. What day is it anyway? He told me he'd asked the knacker to come and take away a horse he had to shoot. We had a fight. He hit me. Knocked me out, as a matter of fact.' She rubbed her jaw. 'When I came round, he was asleep. I took the pony and got out.'

'How far have you ridden?' Dora asked.

'What's the pony's name?' This was important to Callie.

'What are you going to do?' from Steve.

'You got any money?' Ron asked.

'Suppose he comes looking for you?' Slugger's eyes wandered to the antique musket that hung over the fireplace, as if he were considering a siege.

'I don't want to talk no more.' Yaz clamped her mouth shut in her aggressive way, and got up. She looked round the room defiantly and slouched towards the door.

'Where are you going?' Slugger was nervous.

'To take care of my pony.'

'I fed him ages ago,' Callie said, 'and groomed him too. He's got such good manners. What's his name?'

'He don't trust nobody but me,' Yaz said rudely, and went out.

19

THE pony's name was simply Pony. Dora thought that Yaz would move on with him if her father was after them. But that evening, when she came back from a long ride to negotiate with a farmer for a load of hay, Pony was still in the small paddock, and Yaz was in the kitchen smoking the cigarettes that Ron had given her, and playing draughts with Steve.

'Why are the curtains drawn?' They never drew the curtains at Follyfoot, because they were a long way away from anybody, and they liked to see the night, not shut it out.

'Yaz is scared,' Steve said.

'When is she leaving?' The sight of Steve playing draughts cosily with Yaz was extremely irritating to Dora.

'I don't know. She's got nowhere to go.'

'I thought she was on the run.'

'I am.' Yaz leaned back and put her dirty bare feet on the table.

The next day, she wore a sweater and slacks that belonged to Callie, and washed all her clothes and hung them on the trees at the back of the house, because the laundry line could be seen from the road.

'And the pony could be seen too,' she said. 'He's got to be shut away somewhere.'

'There isn't a spare box,' Dora said. 'Steve is creosoting the foaling stable.'

'He can go in that little fenced off bit down in the corner by the wood,' Callie said, 'where I hid Hero when I stole him

74

from the circus. How long are you going to stay?' She was quite thrilled with Yaz, who had brought drama and danger to the quiet farm.

'Depends on what *they* say.' Yaz nodded at Dora, who was examining Pony carefully, looking at his teeth, feeling his clean legs, trying to decide how old he was.

'I'm sorry,' Dora said, with her head under his stomach. 'We can't –'

'I'll work for you,' Yaz said. 'I don't care what I do.'

'We can't afford to pay any more staff.' Dora stood upright and faced her.

'I'll work for my keep.'

'We can't afford to keep another person.' Dora did not know why she felt so antagonistic towards Yaz. She just did. 'Or a horse.'

The girl's eyes filled with tears. 'Come on, Pony.' She took the pony's halter rope, and jerked him rather roughly away.

Three days later, Yaz was still there. She was not much trouble, but she was not much help either.

'For someone who's had a pony for years,' Dora grumbled to Steve, 'she doesn't seem to know much about horses.'

She picked up a rake which Yaz had left lying with the prongs up, and added water to Ginger and Magic's buckets which Yaz had only half filled, since they were the farthest from the tap.

'She tries.' Steve was trimming hoofs, his job while the Colonel was away. He had Wonderboy's hind foot on the leather apron in his lap.

'When she's around. She's usually hiding in the house when there's work to do.'

'She's still afraid of her father. There's no way of knowing if

75

he's hunting for her.' Steve dropped Wonderboy's hind foot and took his file and knife round to start on the other side. 'It's all a bit of a mystery.'

'Yeah,' Dora thought rather sourly, plodding back to the tap with a bucket, the age-old mystery of knowing how to get away with it. The kind of knowledge that Dora had never had.

Dora tackled Ron.

'She's got to go.'

'All right,' Ron said amiably.

'Get rid of her then.'

'Not me job.'

'Someone will have to.'

'What's the matter?' Ron grinned. 'You jealous?'

'She'll have to go,' Dora said to Slugger, who was making soup in the big iron cauldron in which he was stewing together meat, vegetables, potatoes, bread, the remains of the egg pie, to make Slugger soup, a weekly favourite.

'Bit awkward though,' Slugger said, stirring, ''cos she's got nowhere to go and no money.'

'Too bad.' Dora fished a piece of meat out of the soup and ate it.

Slugger slapped her hand, and splashed soup on his shirt. 'Tie the apron on me, there's a love. It's no joke being one-'anded.'

Dora went upstairs and knocked on the door of the spare room, where Yaz was playing the radio she had taken from Dora's room.

'Who's that?' Yaz had a cautious, breathy voice, sometimes hardly more than a whisper.

'Dora. Can I come in?'

'I don't care,' Yaz said uninvitingly.

She was lying on top of the flowered quilt with her shoes on, reading a magazine and eating chocolate.

'Got nothing to do?' Dora asked.

'No. Boring, ain't it?'

'You don't have to stay.' Dora stood in the doorway with her fists clenched.

'You didn't say that to Steve,' Yaz turned her head and looked at Dora shrewdly, 'when he came here with Cobbler's Dream. Wasn't even his pony, was it? He stole him. And he was let stay here.'

'How do you know?' Dora came into the room and shut the door.

'He told me.'

Dora felt pretty bad about that. Steve's past was his secret. She would never tell it to anybody. Why had he told Yaz?

'That was different,' she said. 'Cobby had been blinded in one eye. He was going to be put down.'

'Pony was going to shot. Don't you believe me?'

'I don't know.'

'Suit yourself.' Yaz put up the magazine and pretended to go on reading.

20

THE next day, a police car drove through the gate. A uniformed officer and a plain clothes man walked under the arch into the stable yard.

Dora and Yaz were up in the room over the tack room, putting clean sheets on Steve's bed. When the dogs began to bark, Yaz looked out of the window, then suddenly drew in her breath and shrank back against the far wall, as if an invisible hand had pushed her.

'What is it?' Dora stopped pummelling a large pillow into a small pillowcase.

'Police!' Yaz whispered. Her small face was like a hunted field creature. She looked so terrified that Dora forgot her dislike and doubt. Instinctively she wanted to protect her.

'Get under the bed,' she whispered. 'I'll go down.'

Yaz slid under the half-made bed. Dora went down the ladder to the tack room and out to the yard, trying not to look as nervous as she felt.

'Can I have a word with the Colonel?' The plain clothes man was casual and friendly, as if he had merely come to pay a neighbourly call.

'He's abroad. They won't be back till next month.'

'All right. Just making a – you know – a general survey, who's living where, how many staff you've got, that kind of thing.'

'Let's see, there's four of us working here, three living here, counting the Colonel's stepdaughter, and then there's all the horses. Robin, Cobby, Wonderboy, Hero, Magic, Nigger,

Fanny, Spot, Lancelot – he's the oldest horse in the world –
Ginger, Dolly –'

'All right, all right.' The man in uniform cut her off. 'We'll
take your word for it. No one new in the household then? No
extra stable workers?'

'No.' It was only partly a lie. You couldn't call Yaz part of
the household, and she certainly didn't work.

'Seen any strangers around?'

'No.' Yaz was not a stranger. Dora knew her pretty well
after four days. 'Are you looking for someone?'

'Not really.' The plain clothes man was still casual, bending
to pat an inquisitive dog, whistling at one of the donkeys, who
crossed a corner of the yard on the way to the water trough.
'Just a routine check.'

As they turned and went out to their car, Steve rode in on
Ron's motor bike, with a gallon milk jug swinging from the
handlebars. To save money, they had given up deliveries and
started to collect from the dairy themselves.

'What did they want?' Steve got off the bike.

'I don't know.' Dora had been breathing fast while she
talked to the policemen. Now she felt icy calm and clear-
headed. 'They were looking for someone. I think they were
looking for Yaz.'

'Where is she?'

'Under your bed.'

Dora went back up the ladder. Steve put the bike away and
followed her. Yaz came out from under the bed, coughing,
with fluff in her straw mop of hair.

'Could you hear?' Dora asked.

'Thanks for not telling.'

'Were they looking for you?' Dora asked. 'What is it, Yaz?
What have you done?'

79

Yaz looked from Dora to Steve. Then she sat on the bed and put her face in her hands. 'I can't tell you.'

'You'd better,' Steve said, quite roughly.

'All right, I'll tell you.' Yaz looked up and shook back her hair. 'I killed my father.'

Dora felt as if she had been punched in the stomach. She could not speak.

'Say that again,' Steve said grimly.

'It was like this, see.' Yaz did not look at either of them. 'Night before I came here, it was. He was drunk. Yelling and cursing, and hitting me every chance he got. I hid in my room, but he dragged me out of bed and made me cook a meal for him. It wasn't the way he liked it, so he threw it at me, plate and all. There was a fight then. He came at me with a chair. I ducked, and then he smashed the chair on the stone floor, and picked up the butcher knife. I got hold of a chair leg and I hit out – I didn't know what I was doing. I hit him at the back of the head, and he went down like a stone.

'I waited for a while to see if he'd move. Then I went and looked at him. His eyes were turned up and blood was coming out of his mouth. He didn't seem to be breathing. He was very cold. I couldn't find his pulse. I thought he was dead.'

'What did you do?' Dora whispered.

'Nothing for it but to run. I couldn't stay with – with that. I went and got the pony and got out as fast as I could. I rode and rode. I'd heard about this place – how you take in horses. It was my only hope.'

From the window of Steve's room, Dora watched Yaz leave the tack room, look furtively left and right as if she thought the police might still be about, and dart across the yard to the house.

'What are we going to do?' Dora turned to Steve.

'God knows. We can't turn her in. But harbouring a criminal, that's a crime too.'

'Can you be put in prison for that?'

'Probably.'

'We can't go to prison. We've got to run this place. What on earth shall we do? Tell Slugger?'

'He'd have a heart attack.'

'And I wouldn't trust Ron. He doesn't like Yaz anyway. If only the Colonel were here!'

'We could telephone him,' Steve suggested.

'It wouldn't be safe. Suppose the line is tapped? You can't tell a story like that over international telephone.'

'One of us could go out to him, if we had the money for a plane ticket. Do you think Mrs Oldcastle would lend it to us?' She was the only rich person they knew.

'I doubt it,' Dora said. 'She's turned mean. She was rude to Ron, remember, when he asked her for a donation to Follyfoot. Oh, I wish the Colonel was here!' she said again.

'Well, he's not.' Steve looked at her with his dark steady eyes. 'There's only you and me, Dora.'

When Callie came home from school, spinning her hat in one direction and her book bag in the other, she found Dora in Robin's stable, pulling his mane to thin it and make it lie down. She and Steve had decided that the best thing to do for the time being was to lie low and pretend that nothing had happened.

'What were the police doing here?' Callie demanded at once.

'What makes you think they were here?'

'When Laurie Drew's mother came to fetch her, she said she'd seen a police car in our gateway.'

'It was nothing.' Dora stayed on the other side of Robin, concentrating on back-combing and pulling his mane. 'You know there's been a lot of cars stolen. They thought one of them might have been dumped on our land.'

'How boring,' Callie said. 'All the way home on the bus, I hoped it was something exciting.'

21

THE police did not come back. Yaz calmed down, but Dora was nervous and on edge. Every time a car came down the road, she thought it was the police again. Every time the telephone rang, she jumped out of her skin.

For the umpteenth time, she said to Steve, 'She'll have to go,' and for the umpteenth time, Steve said, 'How can we turn her out?'

'But Steve –' Dora could not get out of her head the picture of Yaz with the chair leg in her small stubby hands, the man crashing to the floor. 'But Steve, she's a murderer.'

'Manslaughter,' Steve said. 'It was in self-defence.'

'Why doesn't she give herself up then?'

'She will,' Steve said, 'when she's ready. You can't make her.'

And for the umpteenth time, Dora wailed, 'I wish the Colonel was here!'

Yaz herself, the cause of all this agony, seemed to be more relaxed now that she had got it off her chest. On Sunday, she said that she was sick of staying in the house, and was going to take Pony out to the woods and look for some ferns.

'I'm interested in them too,' Callie said. 'Do you collect them?'

'I did. Nothing much else to do, living there with my father like that.'

'In the woods,' Callie said, 'if you go down on the north side, there's some quite rare ferns. Wait till I get Cobby ready, and I'll come with you and show you.'

'I'd rather be on my own,' Yaz said. 'I gotta think.'

'It's no fun on your own,' said friendly Callie.

'Pony doesn't like Cobbler's Dream.' Yaz was putting the bridle on the brown pony, fiddling and fussing with the buckles, because she was irritated.

'He does,' Callie protested. 'He likes everybody. You make him out to be so temperamental, but he's one of the easiest ponies we've ever had here, considering what ponies can be like. Look, you've got that curb chain twisted. Why do you ride him in a curb anyway? He doesn't need it.'

'How do you know?'

'I rode him when you were staying in your room.'

'You got no right!' Yaz spun round angrily.

'He needed the exercise. Look, Yaz, the curb's still twisted. You turn it like this, see, laying all the links flat –'

'Knock it off,' Yaz said, 'and give me a leg up.'

'If you can't mount bareback –'

'I gotta bad leg.'

'– how will you get on again after you get off to gather ferns?' Callie heaved her on to Pony's back. 'Better let me come with you, Yaz. You might get lost anyway.'

'Let her alone!' Ron shouted from half way up a ladder, where he was giving the weather end of the barn its yearly coat of paint before the winter. 'She's anti-social.'

As Yaz turned the pony to go out of the yeard, Callie put in a last word. 'Better take a halter if you're going to tie him up anywhere.'

'I'll tie him with the reins.'

'Oh Lord.' Callie swung her head and clucked her teeth like an old woman. 'Oh dear, oh dear, oh dear. Didn't anyone ever tell her?' She fussed and clucked, pushing the stiff broom across the yard, and Yaz gave the pony a slap on the ribs with the flat of her hand and trotted out of earshot.

'Why can't you leave people alone?' Ron hung his paint pot on a bent wire on the top rung and started to climb down the ladder. 'Everybody's got to do everything your way.'

'There's only one right way, with horses.'

'Horses, horses. What about the poor people? I think I'll take some time off on me own as well. I'm worn out.'

As his toe touched the ground, Slugger came out of the barn.

'Back up that ladder, young Ronald.'

'It's Sunday. It's not right to be working on a day of rest.'

'You know why you're working on a Sunday.' Slugger tipped his hat over his eye against the sun and squinted up at Ron sternly. 'To make up for all those mornings you been late to work. Now get on with that job. I want at least half that end done before supper.'

'The paint fumes make me dizzy.'

'I'll give you something that'll make you dizzy.' Slugger shook his fist at him, and Ron went slowly back up the ladder, dipped his brush in the paint and gave it a casual flick.

Slugger stepped back just in time. 'Watch what you're doing.'

'Stand out of the way then,' Ron said grandly. 'There's men working up here.'

But when Slugger had gone into the house for his afternoon nap, Ron came down the ladder again, stepped out of the painting overalls, stiff with years of different colour paint, and went to get his motor bike.

'Where are you going?' Steve asked.

'Just to get some fags. Yaz smoked me last packet.'

It took ten minutes to get to the village and back. When Ron had not returned in half an hour, Steve got out of the chair where he was reading the Sunday paper, climbed into the multi-coloured overalls, which told the story of every colour they had ever used at Follyfoot, and went up the ladder to finish the end of the barn.

Not to help Ron. To help Slugger. When the old man got angry with Ron, his eyes bulged and his face flushed the colour of a radish. He had trouble enough with his broken arm without getting apoplexy as well.

And although Steve did not admit this to Dora, he was dead scared about Yaz. Better to have some work to keep his mind off it.

While he was slapping away with the brush under the eaves of the barn, an extremely elegant woman whom he had never seen before rode into the yard on a tall chestnut horse with dazzling white stockings, impeccable tack, and no sign of the growth of a winter coat, which all the Follyfoot horses were showing.

The woman stopped in the middle of the yard, and looked round with her pointed nose in the air, as if Follyfoot were a sewage farm.

'Hal-loo there!' she called, in a high, clear voice. 'Anybody about?'

Steve came down the ladder and walked towards her in the baggy overalls, which had belonged to someone much bigger.

'Good afternoon.' The woman had difficulty in seeing him, since she kept her nose in the air and her chin tilted above her tattersall shirt. 'Do you have horses here?' she asked, although she could see for herself that there were about twenty loose-boxes, some with heads sticking out in innocent welcome for the grand chestnut horse, and old Flame was pottering about in a corner of the yard, snuffing up spilled chaff like a groggy vacuum cleaner.

'We do have one or two.' Steve grinned, taking in the sleek yellow breeches and boots he could see his face in.

The woman could, if she chose, also see for herself Slugger in his oldest, vilest pair of trousers tucked into muddy Wellingtons, creeping down one side of the yard, with one arm in a cast and sling, and the other pushing an extraordinary contraption made out of the body of a wooden wheelbarrow set on two bicycle wheels with a broom stick for a handle, which Ron had invented so that he did not have to do all Slugger's barrow work.

The woman in the boots looked once, winced, and averted her eyes.

'I'll tell you what it is,' she said. 'I've lost one of my horses. It's my daughter's, as a matter of fact, a bay pony –' she pronounced it poneh – 'common little thing, but she sets store by it. It was out to grass and it must have pushed through the hedge somehow. Ponies are more trouble than they're worth, don't you think?'

Steve grunted. No type of horse was more trouble than it was worth, because it was a horse.

'We've looked everywhere.' The woman looked down at him from her great height on the long-legged horse, raising her plucked eyebrows slightly at the clownish overalls and the paint in his black hair. 'I live a good way away, but I just thought, as a last resort, I'd see if it had wandered over here. It's stupid enough to do something like that.'

'Has he got out before?'

'Not till now, it's too maddening. My groom wants to bring him in to clip and get fit before my daughter comes home for the Christmas holidays.'

'Sorry,' Steve said. 'We've had no ponies wandering round here, but I'll keep my eyes open. A bay, you said?'

'Oh –' the woman clicked her fingers as if the pony were

hardly worth describing – 'sort of nondescript, I suppose you'd call it that. A very ordinary, common little thing. Not up to much, it never was, compared to the rest of the horses in my stable.'

'Mare or gelding?'

The woman laughed down her thin pointed nose. 'Absurd – I can't remember. My daughter calls it Scruffy. She can ride anything in the place – hunters, show horses – but it's a sort of pet to her. She'll give me hell when she comes home, if dear old Scruffy has disappeared, you know how it is.

'Oh yes, I know,' Steve said, as if he had everyday dealings with girls who went to boarding school and gave hell to high-nosed mothers with tight canary yellow breeches and voices like a horse neighing for breakfast.

'I'll give you my card.' The woman produced a visiting card from the pocket of her tailored ratcatcher jacket. 'If you do hear anything about that rotten pony, I'll be obliged if you'd let me know.'

'All right.' Steve looked at the card. It said 'Lady Dillingham Joynes, High Pastures, Lesser Overton-by-Grymsdytch.'

'That's a good boy.' Lady D.J. turned the tall chestnut, striking sparks from the cobbles, and he clattered out under the archway, swishing his exquisite golden tail.

22

Ron did not come back from the village. Steve had not thought he would. Ron had a lot of friends all over the towns and countryside, any amount of places where he could hole up for a chat and a smoke, and conveniently forget what time it was.

Steve had more than half the end of the barn done. Dora was up on the roof, clearing leaves and twigs out of the gutter before he got to the corner. Callie was sitting on the Weaver in the yard, trimming his mane with the hand clippers. He had a skin infection, which was easier to treat if his mane was hogged. Since a lifetime of weaving had left him unable to stop swinging his old head from side to side, rocking gently from one foot to the other, it was easier to trim if you were sitting on his back.

He raised his head, still swinging it, and gave out a cracked neigh.

Other horses took it up before anyone heard the sound of hoofs.

It was Pony, coming back sweaty and wild-eyed, with burrs in his mane and tail and his reins dangling broken round his legs.

'I knew it,' Callie slid off down the Weaver's shoulder to catch him. 'I knew what would happen if she tied him up by the reins. Some people have to learn the hard way. Poor Pony.' She patted him and put him into an empty loose box. 'What have you done with Yaz then?'

She took a bunch of hay and folded it into a figure-of-eight wisp to rub him down, hissing to him like the Colonel did.

'Do you suppose Yaz is in trouble?' Dora called from the roof.

'She's too stupid to get into trouble,' Callie grumbled.

Since she had discovered that Yaz was not only lazy and rude, but did not know enough about horses to deserve to own one, Callie was no longer quite so thrilled with her. 'She's only gone the other side of the little wood.' She looked over the door. 'She'll be back in an hour. Do her good to walk.'

Yaz was not back in an hour. Dora and Steve got in the truck to go and look for her.

'Why bother?' Callie said. 'She'll turn up for supper. That kind always do. Why are you looking so worried, Dora?' She stood on the step and peered into the cab. 'Something's up that I don't know about. Tell me. Nobody tells me anything.' Her constant complaint. 'There is some trouble, isn't there? Is her father after her? It's something to do with the police being here. Let me come with you.'

'It's all right, Cal,' Dora said. 'It's always worrying when a horse comes back without its person.'

'Ought we to tell her?' Dora asked Steve as they turned on to the road.

'Too young,' Steve said, and Callie's head, with the pigtails blowing in the wind, appeared at the open window from the back of the truck where she had hopped in when they said she could not come.

'Too young for what? I'm not half as young for my age as Yaz is,' she said. 'I'm twelve, but I behave like fourteen. Yaz is twenty, but she behaves like fourteen sometimes.' She had to shout against the wind as Steve picked up speed down the hill.

They turned down a rutted lane, and then bumped the truck into a field track at the edge of the little wood. When it

90

became too muddy, they got out and walked across the corner through the trees to the place where Callie had told Yaz she could find the special ferns.

The turf of the hillside sloped down to a marvellous view of the river and the rolling brown arable fields, patched here and there with the bright green of winter wheat, that climbed gently up the other side of the valley.

The autumn colour had faded from the thick trees that marked the river's winding course. Soon all the leaves would be gone, and the brown ploughland frozen into hard chunks, and the birds that were still making Sunday music among the trees would have gone wherever winter birds went when they were not hopping round the back door waiting for someone to shake out the breakfast tablecloth.

'Take a good look.' Callie felt cold in the strengthening wind, and wished she had brought a jacket. 'Next time we come up here, it may be snow.'

The view was fine. It always was. But there was no view of what they were looking for. No footmarks of either Yaz or her pony, no answering voice in answer to the calls they sent out.

'Ya-a-az!' It was a good name to yell. It came out like a shriek of agony. Callie stood and bellowed it out across the valley, and a sad bull bellowed back at her from one of the low-lying farms.

They drove the truck round the nearer lanes for a while, searching and calling, but there was no sign of her. When they got back to Follyfoot, Ron had come back on his bike, and was carrying away the ladder and paint pot, since it was getting too dark to paint.

'Where you all been?' he asked, 'walking out on an honest working man?'

'I did half your job.' Steve got out of the truck, still in overalls.

91

'Ta,' Ron said. 'So that's where me painting knickers was. I been looking everywhere so I could finish me work.'

'Do you know where Yaz is?' Dora asked.

'Gone botanical, hasn't she?'

'The pony came back without her.'

'Probably fell off. I daresay she's used to that. What's the matter?' Ron looked at Dora in the gathering dusk. 'Is something up?'

'No, I just thought she might be lost again.'

There had been times when Dora wished she could tell Ron, who skated round the edges of crime, and had friends who were always in trouble. He might know what to do about murder, or manslaughter. But he was too tricky to trust. Even when he was trying to help, he invented so many complications and secret schemes that you ended up in a bigger mess than you were in already.

Sure enough, just before supper time, Yaz walked in at the gate with a long grass in her mouth and a straggly bundle of leaves and roots in her hands.

'Where have you been?' Callie was going round with feeds. 'You weren't where I told you to go.'

'Did you go looking? Daft. I was all right.'

'Pony came back,' Callie said sarcastically, 'in case you were worried.'

'I guessed he would. Stupid thing broke his reins.'

'Stupid you to tie him up by them,' Callie seethed, but Yaz had walked on without hearing.

She had come back in rather a bad mood. She seemed quiet and depressed at supper, her small pale face sad and old. Callie, remembering about her dead mother and her brutal father, tried to make up for seething at her.

'Where did you go, Yaz?' she asked agreeably.

'Nowhere special.'

Callie had lost her father when she was younger. She could remember that she had wept and sulked and refused to eat or speak for days. It must be even worse to lose your mother. No wonder Yaz sat glumly with her elbows on the table, and a rough answer for everyone.

'What kind of ferns did you get?' She tried again. 'Where are they?'

'I left 'em outside.'

After supper, Callie went out to look. She would get out the Colonel's Encyclopedia of British Wild Flowers, and show Yaz how to identify the plants she had found. Callie did not stay angry with people for long. Knowing what it was to want people desperately to like you, she could usually find some way of trying to like even people she did not like.

The greenstuff that Yaz had gathered was thrown down under the tree with the thick horizontal branch where the swing hung.

There was nothing much. Some ordinary ferns. Maidenhair. Hart's tongue. Spleenwort. Nothing that you could not find in the hedgerows and copses round Follyfoot.

23

Ron did not turn up for work next day. Nor the next, nor the next.

Steve finished the end of the barn, and then he and Dora did the other end as well, since there was plenty of paint, and then Dora took Yaz across the road to paint the crooked shed in which Slugger kept the tools for his vegetable garden, which was threatening to supply turnip greens all winter.

'If Ron has gone for good this time,' Dora said when Slugger came out to supervise, 'that'll solve the staff problem when you go back on the payroll next month.'

'I wouldn't want nothing to happen while the Colonel's away,' Slugger said. 'Better give that door another coat, Yaz, my girl. It's warping. After all, I mean, good old Ron, he's a bad boy, any way you look at it. But he's got a good heart. He's been a bit sarky to you, Yaz, but that's only his idea of a joke.'

'It don't matter.' Yaz sloshed away, scattering paint on to herself and on to the turnip greens at the end of each stroke. She was in a funny mood today, vague and detached, as if she were not quite there.

Had she met anyone when she was off in the woods by herself? Dora and Steve had both questioned her, but she swore she had seen nobody. They had been watching the newspaper and listening to the radio news, dreading to hear about the discovery of a battered body, of fingerprints, of the obvious suspect wanted 'to help with enquiries'.

Nothing. It might be months before Yaz's father was found. She ought to pluck up courage and get away, far away, while she could.

That afternoon, she said she was going to go and look for more ferns.

'I hope you find better ones than last time,' Callie said.

'I was upset about losing the pony. And I had all that walk back. I didn't have time to look properly.'

'Sure you don't want me to come?'

'I told you,' Yaz said. 'No.' She kicked the pony forward.

'Take a headcollar!' Callie called after her.

Yaz turned and put a thumb to her nose. Callie stuck out her tongue, but Yaz had ambled away.

Dora took Robin out to the small field to school him over some jumps. They were going to have a Follyfoot hunter trials in the Christmas holidays, and there would be some pretty hot competition from the tough girls at the pony farm, who would tackle any jumps with their New Forests and Connemaras: over, under or through, whichever way they could get to the other side.

Robin was streets better, but he was still rushing his fences, so Dora was doing some slow work with him. She had set up several low fences, and was trotting him backwards and forwards to calm him down and make him use the muscles of his back.

At first he fussed and pulled, making a great production of a jump that was no more than a garden bench with the back broken off. After half an hour of patient work, he relaxed, and was hopping cleanly over every jump with a completely loose rein. Dora felt as though she was glued into the saddle. Robin always made you feel you rode better than you really did. He was the best horse she had ever had – well, he was the only horse she had ever owned – but he was the best she would ever have, if she lived to be a hundred and married a handsome millionaire who did not expect her to cook or clean or wear skirts, or do anything but ride fabulous horses.

Perhaps she didn't need a millionaire, handsome or ugly. It was enough to have a friend like Earl Blankenheimer, who had given her this marvellous bay horse and still sent her cheques from America every few months to pay for Robin's keep.

Hop, he went over the low poles, hop over the little brush fence, trot a few yards, hop over the logs, turn, trot back, hop over the ditch, back over the rails again, at an angle this time, over the bench, the car tyres and the oil drums, and finally over the sheep hurdles, which were higher, and quite a stiff jump from a trot.

Perfect. Dora leaned forward to stroke his fine black mane down on his neck. He reached for a patch of clover and she nearly rolled off, but he threw her back in the saddle, as he suddenly flung up his head and pricked his ears.

A large brown car had stopped outside, and the heads of a man and a woman had appeared looking over the gate of the field that led to the road.

'Hullo! I say, hullo, there!' The man called out hesitantly.

Dora gathered up her reins and rode towards them.

'Do you live here?'

'Yes. This is Follyfoot Farm. Is there something –?'

The man and the woman looked at each other uncertainly and then the woman said, 'Yes, well, there might be something. May we come in?'

'Of course. Bring your car round into the yard. I'll go through the other way and join you.'

She rode back through the other gate, and put Robin into his loose box with his tack on.

The couple got out of the car. They seemed mild-mannered people, rather thickset and square, both with thin, greying hair and unremarkable faces, wearing the kind of brownish clothes you would not really notice.

'Did you come to see the old horses?' Dora asked.

Callie had been taking round the evening feeds. She always liked to show visitors round. In the fading light, she and Dora began the guided tour they never got sick of:

'This is Cobbler's Dream. He was a famous show jumper once, till he got blinded in one eye. This is Stroller, who used to pull a brewery dray. This old fellow is Hero, who came from a circus, where he was being mistreated. He was too stiff to dance or lie down, you see, but the woman had trained him by cruelty, and he was too scared not to try. This is Ginger, who used to be a milk horse, till some old ladies rescued him, because he was going to be shipped abroad for slaughter. This is Lancelot. Would you believe he is the oldest horse in the world?'

The square people followed them without comment.

'This is poor old Frank, who was found with a terrible dent in his nose where a tight headcollar –'

When they were about half way round, the woman cleared her throat and said, 'It's very nice, I'm sure, but it isn't exactly what we came for.'

'I'm sorry.' Dora shut the stable door on Frank and his famous dented nose. 'Most people like to see the old horses and hear how they came here.'

'Well, we would, of course, if we had more time, but it's just that this visit is for a different reason.'

'Oh.' Dora looked at them. They looked at each other, then down at their plain brown shoes. 'What is it?'

'Well, actually.' The man's Adam's apple took a plunge up and down his neck. 'We're looking for a missing person.'

Dora's heart stopped cold and was instantly frozen in ice. What if they were friends or relations of Yaz's father – somebody who was expecting him somewhere, and he had not turned up and they were looking for him? Why didn't they go to the house in the wood then! Perhaps they had, and found it all locked up as Yaz had left it, with the curtains drawn so no one could see in.

'What –' She leaned against Frank's door. She hardly dared say it. 'What kind of person?'

She held her breath to hear them say, 'An artist', but the man said, 'It's a child. A very beautiful girl with long brown hair.'

Thank God. Dora let out her breath. Yaz was safe for a while yet.

'How old?' Callie asked.

'Fourteen.'

'That's not a child,' Callie said, but the woman went on in a low voice, 'It's our daughter Joan. She's been gone for ages. We're worried sick.'

Dora and Callie looked at each other. First Yaz. Now this Joan. It seemed to be the season for runaways.

'Why did you think she might be here?' Dora asked. 'Is she interested in horses?'

'She always was, though she could never have one. We live in a flat in town. Near the University. My husband is a professor there.'

'I'm sorry,' Dora said.

'Thanks anyway.' The man sighed, his thin grey hair lifting in the breeze, his shadowed eyes showing how many night's sleep he had lost. 'We were just following a vague lead. The police did tell us that they had been here and found nothing, but we thought we'd stop and talk to you anyway.'

So the police had been looking for Joan, not Yaz. Thank God Dora and Steve had not telephoned the Colonel, or tried to borrow money to fly out to him. It was possible that nobody had found Yaz's father yet, lying dead in his own blood on the stone floor of the mysterious house in the wood.

Dora felt a hundred pounds lighter with relief. Then she

looked at the downcast couple, heavy with their own anxiety, and said with genuine sympathy, 'It must be awful not to know where she is.'

Dora had run away when she was thirteen. Although she had only stayed away one night, had her parents lost sleep over her? They had not said so. When she came back, exhausted, guilty, expecting them to fall on her neck with cries of joyous relief, her father had said, without looking up from his book, 'You're late for lunch,' and her mother had said, 'Wash your hands before you sit down.'

When she was older, she had run away again, to Follyfoot, and told the Colonel her parents would not care where she had gone. When he telephoned them, they had said, 'We've been so worried – how could Dora do this to us?', which was what they were supposed to have said the first time. Which proved you never knew where you were with parents.

This lot of parents looked very tired and dejected, so as they turned away from the stable where Frank was quietly chewing on the woodwork – a habit he had acquired when he was abandoned in the tight headcollar without food – she said impulsively, 'If you'd like to come into the house for some tea –?'

The weary faces loosened into smiles. 'It would be nice,' the woman said, 'to sit down for a while and get my thoughts together. We've been on the road since early morning.'

'Come on in.' Dora was glad she had thought of it. 'Slugger will brew you one of his special mugs of tea.'

24

CALLIE went to take off Robin's saddle and bridle and feed him. As Dora led Joan's tired parents up the path to the back of the house, Ron's motor bike came roaring up the hill, through the gate with a scream of tyres on gravel, and under the arch into the yard, where it stopped abruptly, like a bucking horse.

Ron switched off the engine and called to Dora. She took Joan's parents into the house, then ran back to the yard.

'Where's Yaz?' Ron was sitting on the bike, which was giving off a smell of heat and oil, his cowboy boots stretched out on either side.

'She's been gone all afternoon.'

'Where to?'

'Off in the woods somewhere.'

'Oh 'orror.' Ron groaned and put a hand to his forehead. 'This is the last time I'm ever going to get mixed up in any funny business. I mean that, Dora. Cut me throat, I swear it.' He swept a dirty finger nail across the crumpled orange scarf wound round his neck. 'I'm staying away from trouble, and you can have that in writing, *if* you like.'

'What are you talking about, Ron? I've got to go. There's some people in the house having tea.'

'People, what people? Get 'em out of here. We don't want no strangers nosing round.'

'What's going on?'

Normally Ron was cool and cocky, even when there was trouble. Dora had never seen him like this, jittery and scared, with his red hair on end, hanging on to the handlebars of his bike as if it were the only security in the world.

'I've got myself into a right old mess,' he said, 'and all because of you lot.'

'What are you *talking* about?'

'*I know where Yaz is.*'

And then suddenly Dora had a revelation. All the puzzling, mysterious things that had been going on – Yaz's fantastic murder story, her changeable moods, her funny accent, her weird behaviour, right back to the first meeting when she called her pony it instead of him – it was as if a dusky curtain had been pulled back in Dora's brain, and a scene of dazzling clarity revealed.

'Never mind *where* she is.' She hopped up and down with excitement. 'I think I know *who* she is.'

'What's that you say?'

'Some of what she's told us isn't true.'

'Ha!' It was not Ron's old jaunty laugh, but a bitter, jeering sound. 'You only just found that out? I was right then. You was born yesterday.'

'None of it is true, perhaps. She's not even twenty.'

'Ha! Fifteen, more like, if that.'

'Her father isn't mur- I mean, he's not even an alcoholic. Her mother's alive. She cut her hair and bleached it.'

'How do you know?'

'I'm guessing, but it all fits. Her name is Joan.'

'Tell me something I *don't* know.'

'All right, I will. Her parents are here.'

'Don't be daft.'

'Here, I tell you. They're in the kitchen at this very moment, being revived with Slugger's first aid mugs of tea.'

'That's torn it.' Ron beat his brow and left a greasy oil mark under his distraught red hair.

'Torn what?'

Ron glanced round, as if the horses were spies. He swung his leg over the back of the bike, and pulled Dora into the tack room.

Callie was in there with Robin's bridle on the cleaning hook that hung from the ceiling. She was going over the leather with neatsfoot oil.

'Out.' Ron jerked his thumb.

'Not on your life.' Callie stood her ground, with the oily rag in her hand. 'There's too many secrets going on, and I'm fed up with not knowing. Who are those people in the house?'

'Yaz's parents,' Dora said.

'Can't be. Her mother's dead and her father beats her. Oh.' Her mouth drooped. 'You mean it was all lies? She's Joan, not Yasmin? But they said "beautiful".'

'That's parents,' Ron said. 'Listen, I got this friend Mickey, see. Lives down by the canal, near Carter's coal yard.'

Dora had another revelation. In a flash, her mind went back to the first time she saw Yaz, and she thought that she had seen her somewhere before. It had been puzzling her ever since. Now she knew where she had seen that grubby little face.

'The ten mile ride!' she said.

'Ride, what do you mean, ride?' Ron grumbled irritably. 'Listen, Dora, this is serious stuff. We're not playing with gee-gees now.'

'The day of the ride,' Dora went on, 'when we rode through Carter's coal yard to get over the canal bridge, a girl looked out of one of the sheds. Her eyes looked sort of scared, as if she were shut in, or hiding.'

'Well, she was,' Ron said. 'That's what I'm trying to tell you, if you'll just shut up. My friend Mickey, he hangs out with that crowd down there, see. Big operators some of them are. Some are only into the little stuff, like stealing hubcaps and nicking fags. When old Yaz turned up –'

'Where from?' Callie was automatically rubbing the nose-band over and over, staring at Ron.

'From where she lived. That part of it is true. She did run away from her Mum and Dad, who Dora says are in the kitchen, in peril of their lives from being poisoned with Slugger's tea. On the loose, she meets up with Mickey somewhere, see, and for various reasons, not unconnected with the kind if character she is, Mickey latches on to her to do a job for him.'

'Yaz never does any work,' Callie said.

'You've lived with me long enough to know what a job is,' Ron said sternly.

'A robbery?' Dora asked.

'That's about the size of it. Her parents were on the hunt for her, so she had to be hid. Old Carter, he owed Mickey a favour for some special stuff that Mickey had – well – found for him, so he agreed to hide her down the coal yard. The police came. They dragged the canal. Fished up a lot of old boots and a dead bicycle wheel. "What are you looking for, officer?" I happened to be down there that day, and got talking to one of the coppers in my pally way. "A young girl," he says. "There was a rumour she was seen down this way, and we don't want to leave no stone unturned, nor no ditch undredged."

'So after that, it wasn't safe for Yaz to hang about, with all them coppers buzzing round like wasps round the dregs of a glass of beer, so Mickey dreams up this fantastic solution. Hide her at Follyfoot.'

'You knew who she was,' Callie said. 'That's why you were so rotten to her.'

'Sharp girl. Of course I knew. And I knew one sure way to get her taken in here. With a sob story about a horse. So Mick finds her a bridle, and she borrows this pony –'

'Where from?' Callie asked.

'From a field, never mind. Everything was going lovely. Until today.'

'What's happened?'

'Well, old Mickey, he's a car fancier, see. Knows 'em all, including how to start 'em without a key. Detective Sergeant turns up and takes Mick down to the station. Wants to talk to him about some of these four-wheeled pets that have gone missing round the neighbourhood.'

'What's that got to do with Yaz?' Dora asked.

'Everything. Yesterday was the rehearsal. Today's the day of the job. Yaz is already in that house, waiting for Mick to come and give the special signal so she can let him in when the old lady's asleep.'

25

'*What old lady?*' A dreadful suspicion invaded Dora's mind.

'Well.' In the dim light from the tack room lantern, Ron shuffled his feet and looked uncomfortable. 'You know. Her what grows the brussels sprouts.'

'Mrs Oldcastle? But she's a friend!'

'As much as a rich person can be anybody's friend.' Ron had his own set of standards and morals. 'Mean old devil. She's got it to spare, you know. She's never going to miss it – some of that silver and stuff.'

'Well, I'm glad they took Mickey to the police station,' Callie said. 'Now Mrs Oldcastle is safe.'

'But Yaz ain't. Suppose Mickey talks about where she is? Turns informer to save his own neck. If they find Yaz, waiting in that house, she's had it. Not fair really. She's only a silly kid. Not much older than old Cal here.'

'I wouldn't get mixed up in a rotten mess like that.' Callie threw the oily rag in the box and hung up Robin's bridle.

'Yaz ain't had your advantages,' Ron said. 'Brought up too sheltered. She's wild for adventure.'

'It's crime.'

'It's a sort of game to her. She don't understand.'

'But you and Mickey do!' Dora flared. 'It's a filthy trick. We've got to get Yaz out.'

'That's the point,' Ron said. 'I don't know the signal.'

'One of us must get into the house, the same way Yaz did. How did she get in? Mrs Oldcastle keeps that place shut up like the Tower of London.'

'That's the other point,' said Ron. 'You know how tiny Yaz

is. The only way into that house is through a little dog hatch the old lady had made, with a flap that pushes back and forwards, so darling Pookie can go in and out at will. That's why Mickey picked Yaz, because she's got a lot of nerve, and she's narrow enough to get through that door. There's nobody else could do it.'

Callie came and stood in front of Ron with her fists clenched. 'There's me,' she said, and set her jaw.

'No, Callie –' Dora began.

'Why not? I'm no bigger than Yaz, and I've got just as much nerve.'

'You know the old lady's got a gun?' Ron said.

'Oh pooh, an air gun. I'm not scared,' Callie said, although she was.

'Good kid,' said Ron. 'But you've got to swear –'

'Let's get going.' Callie moved impatiently to the door.

'No, listen.' Ron shoved her up against the wall and pinned her there with a large hand across her throat. 'Swear,' he said, as Callie's eyes rolled at him above the dirty hand. 'Swear you'll never tell another soul the deeds of this night.'

Callie made some squeaky, choking noises. When Ron shifted his hand, she gasped, 'How can I swear when you're throttling me? Come on, you're wasting time – let's go!'

It was dark outside, and the wind was getting up. The big brown car had gone.

'Hurry, Ron!' Callie put a leg over the back of the motor bike.

'I dunno.' Ron hung back in the tack room doorway. 'Suppose something's gone wrong, and they've caught Yaz? I can't risk being seen round there.'

'To save Yaz?' In her anger with Ron, Callie had forgotten that Yaz was a cheat and a liar. The adventure was like a crusade.

'What's she to me? Save my skin, that's what I'm thinking about.'

'Get Steve,' Callie told Dora.

'Don't bring him in on this.' Ron grabbed Dora's arm.

She shook him off. 'Why not? *He's* not a coward.'

Steve had spent most of the afternoon trying to make the truck go. Seeing that there was a light in the cart shed, Dora went to find him. He had set the heavy duty torch on a beam, and was still working on the engine, wearing a pair of grimy white overalls that had once belonged to a racing driver he admired.

'Does it work?'

Bending over the engine, Steve jumped as Dora came into the circle of light. 'Hunk of junk. I'll never get it going.' Pieces of the engine were lying about on the ground. They did not look as if they would ever fit back in.

Dora groaned. 'Just when we need it.'

'Who needs it?' Steve stood upright and wiped his hands on one of Callie's old vests. 'We're not going anywhere, are we? Something good on at the cinema?'

'I wish it was the films, but it's real. Listen, Steve, I've got to tell you. Yaz is in bad trouble.'

'She can't be in any worse trouble than she is already.'

'It's all different. I can't explain everything now, but will you take Callie on the back of Ron's bike?'

'Where to?'

'Come on!' She took his hand and began to gabble some of the story at him as they ran across the yard in a spatter of blowing rain.

26

CALLIE loved to ride on the back of the motor bike. It was even better when Steve was up front. It was fun with Ron, but he took the corners so fast that you were never sure that he wouldn't skid on a sharp turn, and the whole bike fly out from under you, while you scraped the side of your face off on the road.

Steve rode just as fast, but he didn't swerve and skid so much, and his waist was more solid to cling to. The back of the racing driver's overalls, as Callie ducked her head to keep the wind out of her face, did not smell or feel as bad as the back of Ron's cracked leather jacket.

As she lifted her head to see where they were, the wind stung cold and raw against her face. Riding through the wood, where the trees leaned inwards to greet each other, the tops of the beeches were wildly agitated in the storm that was blowing up from the valley. As they roared out of the wood and turned the corner into the lane that led past the back of Mrs Oldcastle's house, a great barrage of rain came down in big drops like hail, and was all of a sudden a drenching torrent.

Steve turned into the back drive, and shut off the engine. No sign of a police car – yet. He pushed the bike under a spreading fir tree where it could not be seen.

At the side of the ivy-grown stable was a small fenced paddock in which Mrs Oldcastle put Harold out to graze, where she could see him from the house. The big lumbering cob was not there now, but tied up against the wall, with his head down and his tail tucked in against the rain, Callie and Steve could see the humped outline of Yaz's brown pony.

'She's here!'

There were no lights in the big gloomy house. Its creepered bulk loomed against the stormy sky, water streaming down the slate of the steep turret roofs, the line of chimneys ranged like a battlement.

The old lady must already be in bed. Asleep perhaps, with Yaz waiting somewhere in that darkened house for Mickey's signal to open the door and let him in.

Steve moved closer, crouching through the shrubbery in case there were eyes at any of the darkened windows, where the shades were all half way down, like lowered lids. Callie followed the white overalls, drenched by the wet bushes, one of her sodden pigtails in her mouth to stop herself squeaking when a branch cracked in the storm, or the sudden swaying of a loose creeper looked like someone moving by the house.

At the back of the house, near the kitchen door, was where Ron had told them to look for the dog door. Callie and Steve crept out of the shrubbery, stood upright to get their bearings and made a dash across the soaking lawn to crouch again among the dustbins, listening, waiting, holding their breath for movement inside the house.

Between the back doorstep and the kitchen window from which Mrs Oldcastle had seen poor Kingfisher desecrating her sprouts, they found the little dog door, a narrow flap on a hinge that looked much too small for anyone but a four-year-old to wriggle through.

'Go ahead,' Steve whispered.

'I can't.'

'Yaz did.'

Callie knelt to measure herself against the opening. 'It's too small.'

'Make yourself smaller.' Steve crouched beside her. 'Shrink into your bones. Suck in your breath.'

Kneeling among the eggshells and orange peel that some marauding dog had pulled out of an overturned dustbin, Callie leaned the top of her head against the flap and pushed. The worst part was sticking her head into an unknown room where anything might be lurking. She shut her eyes and pushed her head through, waiting for a blow, the lash of a cat's claws, the barking rush of a dog.

Silence. The ticking of a clock. Nothing else. She opened her eyes. In the faint glow from a pilot light on the gas stove, she saw the cluttered kitchen, dishes and packets of food and saucepans everywhere as she turned her head from side to side, a cheap alarm clock marking time among the shelves full of heavy china on the dresser.

Her head was in, but her shoulders were not. She knelt there like a sinner in the stocks, then pulled out her head.

'I can't get through.'

'Go sideways.'

The flap door was slightly longer than it was wide. By lying down on the wet garbage, Callie could just squeeze her shoulders into the opening. She stuck. For a moment of suffocating panic, she could not go backwards or forwards, then strong hands pushed against the bottom of her Wellingtons, and she was catapulted on to the kitchen linoleum with a dish of stale cat food at eye level, and the alarm clock counting her out.

When the motor bike swerved through the gate and roared off down the hill, Dora could not stand it. If there had been room for three, she would have gone with them. The waiting was going to be unbearable.

The yard was quiet, except for the soft hiss of the steady rain on the cobblestones, and the familiar stamp and blowing of horses busy with their hay. Now that Ron had gone into the house, Dora realized that with all the panic about Yaz, they had forgotten poor Pony, so innocently involved, and perhaps tied up somewhere by his reins without shelter.

There was a way she could get into the drama. She could take Robin and go and look for the pony.

She took his tack out again and saddled him in the dark, adjusting girths and buckles quickly by feel, since she knew the feel of everything about him so well.

As she leaned over the half door to lift the latch, she saw that the back door of the house was open and a shaft of yellow light lit the rain slanting along the path. Slugger sloshed into the yard with a sack over his head, calling for her.

'In here!' Dora stood in front of Robin, so that Slugger would not see that he was bridled.

'What you doing, girl? You spend more time in that stable than you do in the house. Where is everyone? Ron gave me some garbled tale. He's in a state.'

'They went out for a bit.' Dora did not want to embroider a tale that might be different from Ron's.

'Where to? 'Ere.' The old man moved closer, lifting the sack to peer. 'What's that horse got a bridle on for?'

'I'm taking him out.'

'In the dark? It's pouring of rain.'

'Listen, Slugger. Something's up. I can't tell you now, but I promise I will later. Steve and Callie are out somewhere, and I've got to go too.'

'You've not then.'

He put his hand on the door, but Dora pushed it open, led Robin out and climbed quickly on to his back.

"Ere,' Slugger said, as she turned away. 'You can't do that. I'm in charge and I say you can't. 'Ere!' he wailed, as Robin slithered over the cobbles and clattered under the arch. 'I'm in cha-a-arge!'

27

CALLIE scrambled to her feet. Cautiously, feeling her way from chairback to table, along the edge of the cluttered table, and from chairback to counter to wall, she reached the doorway. On the other side, away from the faint glow of the pilot light, the passage was very dark.

She stood in the doorway, peering into what seemed to be a black tunnel, and whispered, 'Yaz?'

Ahead of her, the house settled into the night, with creaks and tiny tickings.

'Yaz?' She had no idea where Yaz would be. Very slowly, feeling her way in and out of the ridges of the wall panelling, she made her way down the black passage. On her right, a wide staircase rose. As her eyes grew more accustomed to the dark, she could dimly see carved bannisters, and ascending beyond them a series of portraits in heavy gilt frames.

She reached the bannister post and put her hand on its smooth acorn shape. Did she dare turn on a light? What was it like to get shot with an air gun? There were two wide doorways on her left, which probably meant switches between. Ahead of her, a high square hall stretched away on either side, a grandfather clock ticking, much too slow, vast shapes of heavy furniture looming, urns, great vases, candlesticks, obese lamps. It was like groping through a museum. Ahead of her was the double front door, with coloured glass on either side, but almost no light coming through on this wet black night, only a finger of ivy tapping. Outside, the wind made organ noises in the gutters, and the trees rushed with sound. By the wall, a man waited for her, with his arm outstretched.

Callie could not run. It was like a dream where you are rooted. When the waves of fear subsided, she saw that the man was rooted too. It was not a man. It was a suit of armour, one jointed steel arm held stiffly out with a silver tray wedged between the gauntlet fingers.

What other terrors lurked in wait for her in this ghastly mausoleum? Suddenly Callie could not bear the unknown darkness any longer. She stretched out her hand to the wall between the doorways, and as her fingers found the switch, a hand was clasped over hers, and her scream was stifled by another hand across her mouth.

It was Yaz's hand. It smelled of the pony. Yaz's voice breathed huskily, 'Shut up, or I'll kill you.'

She dragged Callie through one of the doorways and shut the door softly before she took her hand from Callie's face.

'Get out!' Callie whispered. 'They've got Mickey. You've got to get out of here.'

'Has he talked?'

'I don't know.'

Yaz breathed an oath that would horrify the parents of Joan. Moving like a silent cat, she opened the door again, stuck her head out into the passage, listened, then stepped out.

Callie was more clumsy. Following Yaz, she tripped over a stool, reached out to save herself, and pulled a picture off the wall.

The noise was deafening in the silent house. Yaz slid back into the room, grabbed Callie's wrist, and froze.

A distant yapping became louder, as a door opened upstairs, and the dog's nails rattled on the floor.

'Who's that?' The voice of Mrs Oldcastle, not old and trembly, but strong and unafraid. 'Who's there?'

The dog was barking itself into a frenzy at the top of the stairs.

'Shut up, you fool,' muttered Mrs Oldcastle. She evidently grabbed it by the collar, because it choked on a bark and began a strangled whine. 'Is there someone there? Well, *is* there?' she demanded impatiently, as if almost hoping that there was. 'Because if so, I have to warn you that I am armed.'

Yaz's nails dug into the flesh of Callie's wrist. They held their breath as the creak of a stair told them she was coming down. One creak. Two creaks. Three creaks. Very slowly. Not from fear. From rheumatism. Four creaks.

'Hullo there,' the old lady said in a conversational, matter-of-fact voice. They could hear her breathing, with little laboured whistles, somewhere in the darkness above their heads. 'Well then,' she said to the dog, or to herself, 'I was dreaming. *That's* all right then.'

She must have loosened her hold on the dog's collar, because it let out a sharp bark, muffled as she put a hand round its nose.

'Shut up, I told you. You're dreaming too. You're as big an old fool as I am.'

The stairs creaked again, more heavily, as she plodded back up to bed.

Yaz let go of Callie's wrist, but it felt as if her nails were still there. Without looking to see if Callie followed, she fled down the passage, Callie creeping behind in her Wellingtons, with her hand tracing the panelling.

In the kitchen, Yaz went on her knees, turned sideways and slipped easily through the flap of the dog door. Outside, she gave a little yelp of surprise, and Steve muttered something.

It was easier going out than coming in. Callie must have shrunk from fear. She fell on her face among the garbage, scrambled up and followed Steve and Yaz in a dash across the lawn to the shelter of the dripping shrubbery.

114

Steve gave Callie a nod as she joined them. He looked grim and rather angry, which meant he had been worried. Callie wanted someone to thank her, to say, 'Well done', or, 'Good old Cal', or something like that. But Yaz never would, even though Callie had saved her neck, and Steve did not look as though he felt like it.

Under the fir tree, Yaz swung a leg over the back of the motor bike, but Steve pulled her roughly off.

'You go back the way you came,' he said.

Steve lifted Callie on to the back seat. He wheeled the bike out on to the driveway, swung his leg over and started the engine. Callie put her arms round his waist, laid her head against his broad back and clung on exhaustedly, as he moved away fast.

28

WHEN Callie climbed off the motor bike at Follyfoot, she staggered, feeling as old as Mrs Oldcastle, and twice as feeble. She realized that she was shivering. Had been shivering for quite a long time, probably since that nightmare moment which she would never forget for the rest of her life, when she put out her hand for the light switch and another hand covered it.

Crossing the yard, she went automatically to Cobby's stable. His head with the bold white blaze was already over the door, his nose moving in a silent greeting, his rubbery lips searching her shaky hands for horse nuts.

'I was on a crusade, Cob.' She laid her tired head against his nose.

'Come on, Cal, into the house.' Steve took her hand. As she passed Robin's box, she noticed that the big bay horse was not there. Dora must have turned him out before she went to bed.

Dora was not in bed. She was not in the house at all. In the kitchen, Slugger was asleep in the rocking chair with his feet on the back of a snoring dog.

He opened his eyes when Steve and Callie came in, rubbed them, said 'Hullo' sleepily and smiled without his teeth, then remembered that he was angry with them.

'Pack of lunatics,' he fumed, looking along the mantelpiece for his teeth. 'Dashing off in the rain in the middle of the night like a bunch of wild apes . . .'

Callie went to kneel in front of the dying fire, holding out her stiff hands.

'Did Ron tell you anything?' Steve asked.

'Ron don't tell nobody nothing and I wouldn't believe it if he did. He rang up some pal of his who came to fetch him in a car that smelled of burning mattresses and sounded like the end of the world.'

'Where's Dora?'

'She took off too, the worst of the lot, taking that horse out in the pouring rain with his belly full of oats.'

'Where to?'

'Wherever you was, was all she would say, as she goes haring off and nearly knocks me down. I'm going to write to the Colonel. "It's not good enough," I'm going to say, "Colonel, it's not good enough the way they carry on like a crowd of murderous barbarians the moment your back is turned."'

'I'm hungry,' Callie said in a small voice, from where she crouched by the fire.

Slugger had been too busy raving to notice that she was on the edge of collapse.

'Ah, look at you.' He bent in a motherly way and put the wet straggles of hair back from her pale face. 'Your teeth are chattering. Here's a fine thing.'

He pulled the plaid rug from the back of the sofa and wrapped it round Callie and put her in the rocking chair.

'And what's this?' Rubbing her hands, he saw the red marks of Yaz's nails on Callie's wrists. She pulled them under the rug, and he said, 'Now you sit there, and old Slugger will get you a bowl of hot soup, then it's upstairs to a nice hot bath, and we'll tuck you up in bed and let you off school tomorrow.'

'It's a holiday,' Callie murmured, and fell asleep before he brought her the soup.

She woke as a rush of wind and rain came in at the back door with Dora.

'What a night!' Dora pulled off her soaked anorak and dropped it in a puddle on the floor. 'But Rob and I got Pony back all right. He leads like a dream.'

'Oh poor Yaz.' Steve laughed. 'How did you think she was going to get home?'

'I didn't,' Dora said. 'I was thinking about the pony.' She raised her head like a scenting dog. 'I smell soup.'

Slugger got between her and the stove. 'Not till you tell me what's been going on.'

'It's done with now,' Steve said. 'You'd better not know. You wouldn't like it, and you'd feel you had to tell the Colonel.'

'Because you're in charge,' Dora said sweetly. 'And the Colonel wouldn't like it either.'

Slugger sniffed. But he turned to the stove and ladled out a big bowl of soup for her.

'Come on, me old Cal.' He got Callie up, blanket and all, and helped her out, with his good arm round her. When they got to the door, he turned and said, 'And I suppose I'd better not ask where that Yaz is.'

'That's right,' Dora said. 'Better not.'

Yaz did not come back that night, nor the next day. They did not go to look for her. Ron turned up half way through the morning.

The farmer was delivering hay. Steve and Dora were helping to stack the bales in the high loft at the end of the barn.

'Get up here.' Steve looked down as Ron came into the barn. 'You're hours late.'

'Went to the village and got the letters for you.' Ron always had an excuse. 'Bills mostly.'

'Anything from the Colonel?'

'Dunno. There was an airmail letter, I think. I put it all in the house. Where's Yaz?'

'Disappeared.'

'What happened last night?'

'Everything's all right,' Steve said. 'No thanks to you. How on earth did you get mixed up in a mess like that, against some-one like Mrs Oldcastle?' He glanced behind him, but the farmer was outside on top of the load.

'I told you,' Ron said. 'She's got it to give. She didn't want to give nothing, that time I asked her, did she? So it was doing her a favour, in a way, helping her to do us a good turn.'

'*Us?*' Dora's face appeared at the edge of the loft.

'Yeah – Follyfoot. All I been hearing since goodness knows how long is poor, poor, poor, can't pay the feed bills, can't take in no more horses, got to have Slugger put down. Mickey offered me a cut of the take see, if I'd help him by hiding Yaz. So as I knew how bad we needed the money –'

'But not stolen money,' Dora said quickly. 'Ron, how could you?'

'I thought you'd be proud of me.' Ron looked up at the surprised faces of Dora and Steve, hanging down above him from the floor of the loft. 'I did it for Follyfoot!'

29

YAZ did not come back.

'I'm glad,' Dora said, 'except for not knowing where she got Pony. It must be agony to lose a good pony like that. Well, any pony,' she corrected, so as not to insult the ancient shetland, who was browsing blindly about on the lawn, with his forelock half way down his nose, a legless mass of fur in his winter coat. 'But Pony has obviously been someone's friend. They must be going through hell.'

At the word 'hell' a memory surfaced in Steve's brain. *My daughter will give me hell, you know how it is.*

'Lady Dillingham Joynes,' he said aloud.

'What about her?'

'It's just possible. Nondescript, she said. Scruffy. But if she's got all those high class horses, her standards might be different. And if Yaz came up the valley from the canal through Locksley and round by Grymsdytch, she just might. . . .'

In the Colonel's study, the telephone was half smothered by a jumble of letters and bills and magazines and catalogues that had been dumped indiscriminately on his desk. He liked to sort them out himself when he came back, so that he did not have to read all his bills together, or all the pamphlets about hoof dressing and 'Revolutionary new intestinal agent for the early treatment of strongyles'.

Steve burrowed through the papers, sweeping some of them on the floor, and found the visiting card.

Her ladyship answered the telephone, 'High Pastures,' high in her high nose.

'Mrs – er, Lady Dillingham – er, Joynes?' Steve began, his voice rising to a croak.

'Ah-yaas?'

'That pony you were looking for.'

'Ah-yaas?'

'Are you still looking?'

'Who is that?' she asked suspiciously.

'This is Steve, at Follyfoot. You asked me to keep a look out.'

'Don't *tell* me there's any news!'

'That's why I'm ringing,' Steve said patiently. 'We've got – er, found a pony. He doesn't exactly match what you said. Brown or dark bay, he is, rather good looking. Two white socks and a small star. An old crescent scar on the off quarter.'

'Say no more. That's where it got kicked by one of my thoroughbreds. They absolutely can't stand ponies, you know what it is. Where did you find it?'

'Oh – wandering about.'

'It's been gone for ages. Must be in dreadful shape. My daughter will kill me.'

'He looks pretty good,' Steve said. 'He may have been taken in by someone who took care of him, and then got out again.'

'It's too sickening the way people simply *hijack* other people's livestock, and never dream of telling the police – not that *they're* any use. Please bring the pony over at once,' her ladyship said imperiously. 'Have you got a van?'

'Battery's dead,' Steve said. 'I'll lead him over.'

'And my van is gone for a few days collecting some yearlings. If you'll lead that little wretch over, I'll pay you for your time.'

'I don't want that,' Steve said, and quickly regretted his pride, looking at all the bills on the desk.

. . . . . .

It took him about two hours, riding Cobby and leading the pony.

High Pastures was an impressive affair. A large brick Georgian house with a Jaguar and a Mercedes in the drive, white-fenced pastures, and long stable blocks of immaculate loose boxes on two sides of a yard that looked as if it must be swept every five minutes.

As Steve jogged in at the gate, clipped horses in green and yellow rugs challenged him and the ponies over the newly painted half doors. Pony said nothing. Cobby flung up his square head with its blind eye and gave back the challenge as proudly as if he were not wearing hairy heels and an untrimmed mane and tail.

A girl in a grooming smock came out of one of the boxes and said, 'My God, it's Scruffy. What have you been up to, you bad boy?'

'He's been all right,' Steve said.

'Of course he has, he's always all right.' The girl took the rope to pull the pony away from Cobby, whom he liked. 'Come on, the boss won't half play war with you.'

'Is that the boy with the poneh?' Lady Dillingham Joynes came through an evergreen arch from the garden in a tweed suit like a man's with trousers flaring over glove-tight boots. 'Funny thing, you just "happened" to find him. I've heard some tales about that Collywobble place, or whatever you call it. The Colonel is mad as a hatter.'

'The Colonel's away,' Steve said, 'and the pony wandered on to our land.'

'I suppose that one just wandered in too.' She cast a globular eye over Cobbler's Dream, not looking his best, with his winter coat a bit sweated up, and his thick red mane lying on both sides of his muscular neck. She put out a hand to touch him on his blind side, and he jumped. 'Bit nervous, isn't he?'

'He's blind on that side.'

'Not a bad looking sort,' her Ladyship said, 'under all that wool.'

'He looks familiar,' the girl groom said. 'I've seen that pony before. I've seen him at shows.'

'Open pony jumping,' Steve said, 'before he got blinded. Nothing to touch him.'

'Cobbler's Dream!' Lady Dillingham Joynes exclaimed. 'He won the county championship, before those pushy people with that ham-fisted daughter bought him. I used to know them slightly. Not socially, you understand. There was an accident, wasn't there? And then some boy they'd tried to help stole the pony, and –' She looked up at Steve sharply. 'Was that you?'

'Me? Oh no.'

Steve put on his innocent look and lied, then wished he had not, when Lady D.J. said robustly, 'I was damn glad he did it. It was a good bit of work, getting this good pony away from that little monster.'

The girl put a rope round Pony's neck, and gave Steve back his headcollar.

'Thanks for bringing him over,' her Ladyship said breezily. 'I'm vastly relieved. So please don't be stuffy, dear boy.' She took a ten pound note out of the pocket of her tweeds, rolled it up and tucked it through the browband behind Cobby's ear. 'I *have* heard some tales about your place.' She smiled, and looked quite different. 'And I like what I hear.'

Yaz never did come back. She had disappeared for ever, as strangely as she had come.

Much later, long after the Colonel and Anna had come home, a letter came 'To all you lot', in a careless, scrawled handwriting, without a return address. Inside was a small passport-size

123

photograph out of a machine, a child's narrow face, framed by long falling dark hair.

'This is what I used to look like. Will again, when my hair's grown out and the colour grown back in. I got a lift in a car that night. It was going towards where I live, so I thought I might as well go home, cuz I was hungry. I'm back at school now, what a drag. So wot else is new? I may stow away on a boat to Canada. I've got this friend, she knows a person who would give us jobs cooking in a lumber camp.

'Thanx for everything. Luv Yaz.'

30

THE storm that had blown so fiercely on the night of Callie's crusade, had not gone away. It was only going round in circles. Some time later, it came back with full force, and dumped four inches of snow on the hills.

When they were turned out in the morning, the horses went wild with joy. Even the very old ones bent their stiff knees and flopped down with a grunt to roll in the exhilarating whiteness, getting up with icing on them to lurch away with feeble bucks and squeals.

Robin, who had been used to deep snow in America every winter, rolled thoroughly, over and back and over, squeaking the snow beneath him, galloped in a trail of smoke down to the far fence, stopped, snorting, with his head and tail up like a stallion, then dropped his head and pawed at the snow in a businesslike way to get at the grass underneath.

The snow had been the storm's last message. The sun was out in a sparkling sky, and two days later, the snow had melted. It was almost like spring, although winter was only beginning. Dora grew restless. The routine of the work of the farm seemed dull after the excitement of the Yaz adventure.

'Let's do something,' she urged Steve. 'Let's go somewhere. Another big ride.'

'Not with all those kids and ponies,' Steve said.

'All right, just us. Let's go a long way. Somewhere we've never been.'

They decided to ride up into the hills towards the sea, stay the night with an uncle of Dora's who had a farm, and then back across the corner of the moors.

Slugger had been to the hospital to have his plaster cast off, and was able to use his two arms again. Callie recruited some horse-mad girls from school to help with the work. Ron swore on his life – 'for what that's worth' – to turn up on time, even on Sunday. Scared by the hazards of the Yaz affair, he also swore that he was going to stay away from Mickey and the coal yard gang. 'Better to die of boredom than be shot by Mrs Oldcastle.'

The long ride was lyrical and wonderful. Steve and Dora left very early in the morning, clattering through the village while everyone was still asleep. When little Toby at the pub heard the hoofs, he opened the window of his room under the roof, leaned out and shouted, 'Where you going?'

'A long way!'

'You coming back?' In Toby's insecure world, anything might happen. His father or his mother took off from time to time, after fights. He never knew when people might disappear.

'Back in two days!' Dora shouted.

The window below Toby's was flung open, and the furious red face of his father looked out with his hair and beard on end. 'Stop that row and let people get some sleep!'

'Good morning!' Dora waved happily, and they trotted on. Surely the whole world would not mind waking up if they could share in this happiness.

They rode all day, over the broad top of the hills, and down a long wooded slope, out to flatter land, where the wind had some salt in it, coming over the wide pastures from the sea.

The light was going from the sky and the warmth from the air, as they came to the farm where Dora's Uncle Fred had lived for years. He was her favourite uncle, the one her family did not think much of, because he had never achieved the kind of things they thought were important.

He was poor and shabby, barely scraping a living off the land he had bought long ago when he brought his new wife to live here. He had done quite well, but he only had a couple of shire horses now, and a few cows that he kept more because they were old friends than because they gave a lot of milk. By renting some of his grazing, and with his chickens and vegetables and big apple orchard, he just had enough to live on.

Since his wife died, Uncle Fred had slowed down, and was letting things go peacefully to pieces. He lived like a hermit in the kitchen, with the other rooms shut up. His bed was at one end of the low-beamed room, an ideal arrangement, since he could go to bed with the fire still burning.

After Uncle Fred's stew, which was full of onions and carrots and turnips and lumps of good fat bacon, they went out to look at the horses.

They had stabled Robin and Miss America in the huge barn, where Uncle Fred kept his cows and goats in deep litter. They found the horses standing close together at one end of the barn, as if this were their first day at school, watching the somnolent cows from a distance.

'Perhaps we should have some cows at Follyfoot.' Dora relished the milky, acid smell of the cows, who were lying down with their girlish lashes lowered.

'You can have those two old girls, if you like,' Uncle Fred said. 'The yellow ones. Neither one of them has been in milk for a long time. Too old to calve any more, they are.'

'Why do you keep them?'

'Because they've always been here, I suppose.'

Dora squatted down and lifted the cow's heavy head, with its square slobbering nose and dished-in face. Chewing cud, the cow opened big lustrous eyes and looked at her without the curiosity of a horse.

'Would they go in a horse box?' she asked

'Dora,' Steve warned.

'Why not? The Colonel said no more horses, but –'

'He didn't say no more cows. I know. But we don't need two more hay burners.'

Dora patted the knob of curls at the top of the cow's head. 'I wish . . .'

'I used to wish I had money,' Uncle Fred said sensibly, 'but I didn't get any, so I stopped wishing. That didn't get me any either, but it saved me a lot of energy.'

The horses went even better on the way home. Miss America flagged a bit on the last few miles, but Robin was stepping out as bold as ever, his ears keen, his large blue eye taking in every aspect of the scenery. On a ride, he did not behave as if it was just a job. He seemed to enjoy himself as much as Dora did.

It was dark when they got home, and there were lights in the stable.

Callie came running out, as if they had been gone for weeks, followed more slowly by Slugger. She looked over the horses critically, and led Robin to his loose box, where she had put down a deep, clean bed.

'How was your Uncle Fred?' she asked.

'He's nice,' Dora said. 'We slept in the kitchen on mattresses on the floor, because the rest of the house was so cold. He's got cows and chickens and goats and a pig and some pigeons and two dogs and a pack of mangy cats. He wants to give us two old cows. Do you think they would travel all right in the horse box?'

'Don't listen to her,' Slugger called from Miss America's box next door. 'There's not going to be one new animal at this farm when the Colonel gets home next week.'

'Well, that's a pity,' Callie said, going over Robin with a stable rubber, 'because there's a girl in my class, her mother's sending her away to school because she's unmanageable, and she asked me if we could take her pony.'

'No.'

'It's a show pony, and it'll get unmanageable too, if there's no one to ride it.'

'Forget it.' Slugger came into the doorway, carrying Steve's saddle. 'And you forget cows, Dora, and goats and pigs too, while you're at it. Please everybody, please do try not to take in anything, beast or human, before the Colonel gets back.'

31

WHEN the Colonel and Anna flew back, they were to stay one night with the Colonel's brother near the airport, where they had left the car.

That night, the telephone rang late.

'Colonel!' Dora said. 'Oh, it's good to hear your voice.'

The voice sounded rather nervous. 'Yes – hm – ha –' he always did badly on the telephone. 'And yours, my dear. I – er, look – listen, is Steve there?'

'He's in his room. Shall I get him?'

'Don't bother. Give him a message, will you? Ask him to – er, well, to – er –' He was doing even worse than usual '– to bring the horse box,' he ended in a rush.

'What for?'

'Oh, I – er, I've got some stuff to bring home.'

What on earth could it be? The Colonel did not normally go round Italy collecting antiques.

It couldn't be a horse.

It was. When Steve came home with the Colonel, Cobbler's Dream called out a greeting from the field. Something of the same species answered from inside the horse box.

Dora, Callie and Slugger started towards it from various corners of the farm.

The Colonel looked out of the window, with a cheerful grin on his tanned face.

'Colonel –' Slugger began.

'I know,' he said. 'I know. But yesterday when I was with my brother, he told me about this – er, this sort of pony he'd heard was being kept in a filthy shed near his house. Belonged to a junk dealer, but his legs have gone west. He can't be driven any more, but the junk man seemed to think he could. So, I – er, don't you see – bought him.'

'Quite right,' said Dora, and Callie said, 'Oh good,' and Slugger said, 'Of course you did.'

Callie opened the side door of the box and went in to untie the pony. Steve and Dora let down the ramp of the box, and a sorry specimen of junk dealer's pony tottered out backwards, with broken feet and swollen joints, pitifully gone over at the knees, with a ribby pot belly hanging like a hammock from his starved hip bones.

The Colonel dropped his arm across Slugger's shoulders, and they stood side by side and watched Callie lead the pony slowly across the yard, back legs wobbling like loose wheels, his long ears flicking bravely back and forward to the new sights and sounds.

Steve took Spot out of his box, and led him down to double up with his pal Hero, both veterans of the circus. Callie took the pony into Spot's box, where he staggered straight for the empty manger.

'Bran mash?' Dora asked the Colonel.

'With a bit of linseed and molasses – only a handful of oats for now. And you may as well start the vitamin extract right away.'

Slugger sighed under the Colonel's arm.

'It's just that we've been so careful,' he said. 'I was so proud of not having any new customers when you came home.'

'So you should be,' the Colonel said. 'More room for this poor fellow. Don't worry.'

'It'll be all right,' Dora said, going off to the feed shed. 'It always is.'

· · · · ·

When Dora took tea into the Colonel's study, she found him sorting through the mass of paper on his desk.

'Bills, bills, bills. It's hardly worth coming home.' Seeing Dora's face, he smiled quickly, and added, 'You know I don't mean that. It's marvellous to get home, even to all this mess. Looks as if one of the pups has been in here.' He bent to pick some envelopes off the floor. 'What's this? Here, it's for you. Haven't you seen it?'

The airmail letter Ron had brought the day after the Yaz adventure. By the time they had finished storing the hay, with scratched skin and dry, dusty throats, Dora had forgotten all about it.

It was from her friend Earl Blankenheimer in America. The regular amount he sent for Robin's keep. Regular amount! The figure on the cheque was much more than he usually sent. It had a comma and another nought tacked on.

'Had a great bit of luck,' his letter said. 'My firm got the contract to build the new country club, so I want Follyfoot to share in my good fortune.'

'There you are, you see.' Dora handed the cheque to the Colonel. 'I told you it would be all right.'